WALT DISNEY'S

Annette

THE DESERT INN MYSTERY

Authorized Edition featuring ANNETTE,
star of motion pictures and television

By

Doris Schroeder

Illustrated by
James Schaeffing

DISNEY
PRESS

NEW YORK

Contents

CHAPTER 1

Holiday Plans

It was the Friday afternoon before the start of the Easter week vacation. Outdoors, the California sky was clear and blue, and the warm breeze sweeping down from the Hollywood hills was sweet with wild mountain lilac.

Annette parked her white sports car, the Monster, outside the familiar Choc Shop a block from her school. She could hear the usual happy babble of voices inside. They sounded excited today, even more than usual. She knew it was because everyone was looking forward to the week of freedom.

Annette had some plans of her own but they hadn't worked out, though she had tried hard to make them happen. Now she had to go in and tell her best friend, Lisa Kerry, that she wouldn't be going along to Arizona to visit Lisa's family, after all.

Instead, Annette would probably be doing what she had done every year: spending the holiday week at the beach. Uncle Archie and Aunt Lila had a pleasant big old house there that they let her fill with her school girlfriends for Easter vacation. And until this year, Annette had been very happy with this arrangement. She and the girls had always had a good time, even if it was always the same sunning and swimming all day, giggling and gossiping half the night.

Uncle Archie, an old bachelor, and Aunt Lila McCleod, his widowed sister, had made a home for Annette after she had been orphaned several years ago. They were kind and indulgent, but every now and then Uncle Archie would decide that Annette had been getting her own way too often and needed to have a little more managing.

When that happened, Aunt Lila and Annette both took it meekly. Soon Uncle Archie felt that he had done his duty and could relax, and everyone was happy once again.

As she paused outside the Choc Shop, Annette wished she didn't have to disappoint Lisa. Lisa had been her best friend at school ever since the tall, quiet girl with the freckle-sprinkled cheeks and the clear blue eyes had started to attend the same classes last fall.

When she had become friendly with the shy Arizona girl and listened to Lisa's wistful and homesick stories about her desert home, she had decided that Lisa's part of the country was one of the places she wanted to visit first. The spring vacation seemed to offer just the right chance.

Lisa had been planning a trip home ever since Christmas. She hadn't been able to go home then, because she had had a lot of extra studying to do. She had since caught up on her schoolwork, in spite of having to work a couple of hours after school every day to help pay her school expenses.

Of course, Annette hadn't asked right out for an invitation. She had waited till they were doing their homework together in the library one night.

"I don't want to go to the beach again this vacation," she had said, pouting. "It's always the same old thing every year. I think I'll tell Aunt Lila I'd rather spend the week somewhere on the desert for a change."

"Why don't you come home to Pine Mesa with me?" Lisa had asked eagerly. "Mom would be delighted."

"Do you really think so?" Annette had asked hopefully.

"Of course! I'll write her tonight you're coming. She'll be sending me the train fare next week, so I can leave here Sunday morning. We go as far as Williams on the train, and then Dad will pick us up in his truck to go the rest of the way."

"Wonderful! I'll tell Uncle Archie and Aunt Lila and get my ticket first thing tomorrow!"

But Uncle Archie had proved to be in one of his stern moods. "You," he reminded Annette severely, "have already drawn your allowance up to and including June first."

Which was perfectly true, though Annette had been hoping he wouldn't remember it just then!

"You may have your weekly school lunch money, as usual," he had told her, "but unless it's for a grave emergency, no more. That's final."

Annette's tragic expression hadn't softened Uncle Archie one bit. And he had forbidden Aunt Lila to lend her the money, though she wanted to. A vacation trip was not an emergency, as he sternly pointed out.

Annette was always honest with herself. She hadn't blamed her uncle much for refusing. After all, she *had* been extravagant last winter, buying a whole new ski outfit for the Christmas ski party at Mountain Lake. But she had had a wonderful time in the snow, and after all, she could wear the ski togs again many times.

She and Lisa had felt sad about Annette having to give up the trip. But Annette had had a sudden idea. "Hey! I know what! We'll drive down in the Monster! It won't cost us much. Just a few dollars for gas and oil and a hamburger along the way. I know we could manage!"

"Annette! You're a genius! I have almost nine dollars tucked away. Would that be enough?"

"More than enough!" Annette had assured her merrily. "I have nearly ten dollars myself in my silly old piggy bank. We're in!"

"I'll write Mom that she doesn't need to send my train fare, after all!" Lisa cried. "I think she may be kind of glad, at that. Her last letter said they were a bit short of money, but she was sure they could scrape up enough for my fare and she did want me to come home to see what Dad has been doing at the old stage station."

"Stage station?"

"Where the stagecoaches used to stop overnight at Pine Mesa when the Navajo occupied the land. Dad's bought the old adobe buildings and he's remodeling them into an old desert inn, with loads of atmosphere. Mom says it should put Pine Mesa right back on the map, once the tourists find out about it."

This time it was Aunt Lila who had put her foot down firmly. She refused to let Annette start off on the long trip into new, strange country without an older and very reliable person going along to see that nothing happened to the two girls.

At first, it hadn't seemed as if it would be much of a problem to find a suitable person to chaperone them. Many of Aunt Lila's friends liked to travel and wouldn't have minded keeping an eye on the girls. But none of them had planned on a desert trip so early in the year.

And that was that. Now Annette had to break the news to Lisa—and it wasn't going to be easy.

She went on into the Choc Shop, pretending to be as happy and lighthearted as usual, and when her friends called to her out of the milling mob of kids, she told them, "Be with you as soon as I talk to Lisa!" and hurried toward the far end of the counter where Lisa worked.

It was Lisa's job to get out the orders for the regular waitresses to deliver to the customers.

When Annette reached the end of the counter and slid onto the nearest stool, Lisa was carefully concocting an elaborate ice-cream order.

"Hi!" Annette grinned at her friend. "Busy little bee, aren't you?"

Lisa turned eagerly to Annette. "Has your aunt found anyone yet?"

"Nope," Annette answered gloomily, "and I'm afraid she isn't going to. Everyone she has thought of so far seems to be going to Alaska or Mexico City or something. We're just plain sunk, Lisa."

Lisa frowned. "Then she's given up?"

Annette nodded grimly. "I guess you'll be going by yourself, after all."

Lisa wiped the counter slowly before she answered: "I won't be going."

"I thought you were planning to take the train!"

"I wrote Mom not to send me the fare," Lisa explained. "So she didn't." She tried to smile, but it wasn't very convincing. "So I'll be staying right here next week."

"It's all my fault!" Annette said miserably. "I had to go and mess up your plans by wishing myself along. Now I've spoiled your vacation."

"Goodness! You had no idea what was going to happen. You thought everything would be all right, the same as I did. Don't blame yourself."

"Can't you send a wire tonight and tell your mom we won't be able to drive down, after all? She could telegraph the money."

Lisa shook her head slowly. "She'd have to wait till Monday when the bank opened at Pine Mesa—and then by the time I got the wire and cashed the order and bought the ticket, it would be too late to go home. I'd only have a couple of days there before I'd have to start back. It would be a waste of money." Lisa saw how downcast Annette still looked. She touched her hand across the counter. "The only thing I'm really sorry about is that you're going to miss our super-duper wildflowers!"

"Wildflowers on the Arizona desert? Who's kiddin'?" The gangly young man who had pushed his way through the mob was Jinks Bradley, who lived next door to Annette.

"Hiya, Jinks!" Annette was surprised to see him. Jinks's after-school hours were usually spent in the school library. He was an A student in just about every subject, and editor of the school monthly. But he was also known to be so shy that he was usually almost tongue-tied when there were girls around. Now he was trying to joke with Lisa!

"Come and see for yourself sometime if you

don't believe me!" Lisa tossed her head saucily and made a cute face at Jinks.

Jinks gazed at her owlishly through his thick lenses and cupped his chin in one palm. "Wish I could!" he said earnestly. "But I never have that much luck."

Annette was startled. Why, he seemed to mean it! She felt a surge of sympathy for poor Jinks. She remembered that his life, according to Aunt Lila, was pretty much laid out for him by his aunt, Letitia. Jinks was an orphan like Annette, and Aunt Letitia was his guardian. She was a successful painter who specialized in highly commercial subjects like landscapes and flower studies. And Jinks spent practically all his school vacations acting as her chauffeur to whatever scenic spots she decided to paint next.

Aunt Lila, who had no spectacular talents, stood in awe of Letitia Bradley and admired her immensely. "Tish" Bradley was the reliable, self-sufficient type, equal to any crisis.

Annette blinked suddenly. Why hadn't she

thought about Aunt Tish before? She'd be a perfect chaperone!

She waited till Lisa had hurried away toward the front end of the counter to gather up some dishes. Then she tugged at Jinks's sleeve. "Jinks, I just had an idea!"

Jinks turned to her with a dreamy, faraway expression in his eyes. He had been watching Lisa. "Huh?"

"Where are you going next week?"

Jinks looked gloomy. "Where do I ever go except some neck of the woods where Aunt Tish thinks she can find some scenery to paint?"

"But where this time?" Annette persisted.

"Same place as last time. Carmel and the Monterey coast, so she can paint some more twisted cypress stumps. They sell like hotcakes!" He sounded bitter. "Boy! Do I ever get fed up with cypress trees and surf dashing on rocks!"

"Maybe you could talk her out of them for this once," Annette suggested. "Want to try?"

"I dunno." He looked at her doubtfully. "What's the angle?"

"Well, if you coax her real pretty, I bet we might all end up at Pine Mesa, Arizona, looking at those wildflowers that Lisa was talking about!"

Jinks stared at her blankly a moment; then his face was wreathed with a broad grin. "Go on! I think I'm getting the drift! You mean, wildflowers instead of cypress trees?"

"That's the idea. You see, Lisa and I planned to drive down for vacation, but Aunt Lila lowered the boom, unless we could scare up a chaperone. And there don't seem to be any candidates."

"Say no more!" Jinks grinned at her and swung off the stool. "You've got your chaperone! Tell Lisa to start packing."

"But wait. How will we know — ?"

"Don't leave! I've got an angle! Wait right here till I call!" He was away, bucking the crowd like a fullback in the last half of the Big Game.

And a moment after, he had disappeared. "Where did he go?" Lisa was back with an armful of dishes. She looked around for Jinks with a disappointed expression.

"Oh!" Annette teased. "He had to attend to

something much more important than hanging around here!"

Lisa's blue eyes flashed. "Really?"

Annette couldn't keep it up. She laughed. "Want to hear some news?"

"I suppose so." Lisa tried to act as though she didn't care much one way or the other.

"We're going to drive to Pine Mesa, after all!"

"Who says so?" Lisa looked astounded.

"Jinks!" And she explained.

"But how does he know his aunt will change her plans?" Lisa asked.

"I don't know—but he's a brain! And my money's on him, 'specially when it seems to mean so much to him to see those wildflowers of yours!"

Nearly an hour later, the phone rang. Annette dashed to answer it.

"Annette?" Jinks's voice rose almost to a squeak in his excitement. "We go! Aunt Tish is over, settling the details with your aunt right now, and everything's rosy!"

"Wonderful!" Annette shouted, waving and nodding to Lisa behind the counter. "Okay!"

CHAPTER 2

On the Way

There were a few details that had to be settled right away, of course, like finding out when Aunt Tish thought she'd like to get started for Arizona. So Annette hurried home, and Lisa went to her room to pack and wait for Annette's call.

Aunt Tish turned out to be most enthusiastic about the change of plans. "I've always wished to capture the real soul of the desert on my canvas," she told Aunt Lila over a cup of chocolate in the McCleod living room.

Annette and Jinks had their heads together over a road map.

"You're a genius!" Annette whispered happily.

Jinks beamed at her. "How about doing me a favor while you're feeling grateful?"

"Strings, huh?" Annette looked at him quizzically.

"Just a little one," Jinks assured her. "When we start out in the morning, you might sort of suggest that Aunt Tish might be more comfortable in your car than mine. Mine's pretty crowded by the time she gets all her painting doodads loaded in."

"Besides," Annette said with a twinkle in her eye, "you'd rather have other company. Huh?"

"Well . . . kinda!"

She saw that he was actually blushing. "I'll see what I can do," she promised.

But at six the next morning, when both cars were loaded and ready to start, Annette didn't have a chance. Aunt Tish was in command, booming out orders to her nephew and the two girls alike, and before Annette could suggest a more comfortable seat in the Monster, Aunt Tish had climbed into Jinks's car and was wedged in with her easel, paint box, and other paraphernalia.

"Got to get used to roughing it," she called to Aunt Lila and Uncle Archie, who stood in the driveway watching the departure. "Everybody says the best scenery down there is 'way off the paved roads. Might as well get toughened up before we get there. Let's roll, boy!"

At first, they moved through the green, fertile valleys of southern California. They passed long, winding irrigation canals that carried the life-giving water that made the former dry desert land bloom with the choicest of vegetables, cotton, and early fruit crops.

Soon there were wide patches of lupine and California poppies, startling contrasts of blue and gold under the brilliant sky. In the distance now, they could see the hazy outline of mountain ranges, some of them as far away as Mexico.

Aunt Tish was amazed to see the flowering of the desert, and in spite of Jinks's suggestion that they had a long way to go to Pine Mesa, she called a halt, climbed out of the car, and went to work with her sketch pad.

Annette drew up behind Jinks's car and got

out to watch. But as Lisa started to follow her, Jinks hurried to the car and draped himself over the door as he pointed out the far-off mountain range to her.

"Those," he informed Lisa, "are the Chocolate Peaks."

And Lisa, who knew the Chocolate Peaks were to the north and not to the south where he was pointing, let him think he was right. She was happy to be going home and, after all, Jinks had made it possible. So why make him feel small by spoiling his little pretense?

It was a pleasant interlude for both of them, a chance to get acquainted. And Annette, seeing it, kept Aunt Tish from finishing the sketch as quickly as she might have done.

"Did you have to study a long time?" she asked. Aunt Tish laid aside her sketch pad while she went into the story of her progress as an artist.

"When I took up my studies in Paris . . ." Aunt Tish was enjoying herself. It wasn't often that a young girl like Annette took such an intelligent interest in art.

"Aunt Tish!" Jinks had come up with Lisa. "Lisa thinks we'd better start again soon. We have a long way to go and she thinks it would be better to get to Pine Mesa before dark. The spring floods may have made some of the road pretty bumpy."

"But your aunt was just telling me the most fascinating things about her work!" Annette had seen her chance to do Jinks that little favor. "Tell you what! Why don't you and Lisa go on in your car and I'll bring Aunt Tish. I want to hear more about Paris."

Jinks's eyes brightened behind his thick lenses. "Say, that's a good idea! How about it, Aunt Tish? Annette's car rides a lot easier than mine, too!"

So that's how it was arranged. Everyone was happy, including Annette herself, who found to her surprise that Aunt Tish could be quite amusing company, telling about her carefree days as a student abroad.

Soon they were crossing the state line and bowling along a wide concrete highway through the desert. It was a different desert, this time with cactus giants lining the road and making their own special show of brilliant blossoms perched on the ends of uplifted spiny arms.

As they came through the wide desert spaces, the tiny towns were becoming fewer, the stretches between longer. And little by little, the road was climbing into the high plateau country.

It was in the drowsy small town where the road forked north to the Grand Canyon and east to Indian land, that Jinks pulled in at a service station for more gasoline. He waited at the edge of the road and signaled Annette to stop there also.

"Lisa's phoning the Pine Mesa Hotel to reserve us rooms, Aunt Tish," he explained. "She thought she'd better, because when she wrote her mother to expect her and Annette, she didn't know we'd be coming, too."

"Good!" Aunt Tish stretched and stifled a yawn. In spite of the Monster's softer cushions, it was still a long ride. "I hope that hotel has comfortable mattresses."

"Lisa says it's the best in town," Annette assured her.

Lisa hurried toward them, wearing a puzzled expression. "All set," she told Jinks and Aunt Tish. But as soon as Aunt Tish went into the coffee shop to buy souvenir postcards and Jinks started fueling the cars, Lisa confided in Annette. "I'm worried. I asked Mr. Dunlap, the clerk at the hotel, to send his little boy across the street to get Mom."

"Wouldn't he do it?" Annette was indignant.

"Oh, he sent him, all right. But the boy told him that Mom wasn't there, and that Marie, our Navajo cook, said she'd been at the hospital all day. The *hospital*!"

"Why should that worry you? Maybe she's been doing the same as Aunt Lila does. She gives a day each week to helping out at the hospital in Hollywood."

"Oh!" Lisa looked relieved. "I hadn't thought of that. She might be helping old Dr. Marlow, at that. He has the hospital right in his own home, a couple of blocks down the street." She laughed. "When he has more than two patients there at a time, the poor old darling has his hands full. And he never can keep a nurse, with his short temper!"

"You see? Nothing to worry about when you think it over," Annette said.

"I guess not." Lisa laughed again. "I just had a feeling—no reason at all—that something had happened to Dad. . . . He's been working so hard there at the stage station, ever since he got a little short of money and had to let some of the workmen go."

She had almost forgotten her fears by the time they had all finished off their sandwiches and coffee and were ready to roll on again.

"We're about a hundred miles from home now," Lisa told them as they walked toward the two sports cars. "We could save twenty-five miles by taking that dirt road. It cuts across a corner of the big Navajo Reservation."

"Let's take it," Annette said promptly. She could see that a little worry still lingered in Lisa's mind about the reference to the hospital.

So they headed onto the dirt road, which was winding but rather smooth, and started across the red sands of the barren country reserved for the use of the Navajos.

Before they had gone a mile, they were climbing through deep-cut gorges, along the edges of tall mesas, and plunging again to the rocky floors of canyons whose steep sides reached straight up hundreds of feet toward the sky.

For once, Jinks drove with strict attention to the winding narrow road, and behind him Annette did the same, wishing that she hadn't been so eager to try the shortcut.

She hoped fervently that the road would straighten out and get nice and flat soon. It had been a long drive from home and she was tired.

Now they were skirting the side of a steep canyon where the road was scarcely wide enough for two cars to pass.

Hope we don't meet a truck or something, Annette thought uneasily. Up ahead she caught a glimpse of Jinks's car as it made a turn and disappeared again.

Beside her, Aunt Tish, eyes closed and teeth clenched, was hanging onto the side of the seat.

If the car was going to fall off that road, Aunt Tish didn't want to see it coming!

Then, over the sound of her own motor, Annette heard a motor being gunned behind her, and a moment later a horn blasted loudly.

She took a quick look. A car was approaching fast, a big car with the top down. There were two men in it, and one of them, the driver, wore a red beard—that was all she had time to see before the car crowded past her so closely that it almost scraped against the side of the little sports car. Another six inches and it would have sideswiped the Monster and flung Annette and Aunt Tish several hundred feet to the bottom of the canyon.

Then it was gone around the next turn, its rear wheels almost going over the edge.

Annette pulled her emergency brake on and the car stopped. She was trembling from head to foot.

All she could think of was Jinks and Lisa in the little car ahead. Would they be flung over the edge by the crazy driver?

She sat limp, listening for the horrible crash she expected to hear any second.

CHAPTER 3

Trouble at Pine Mesa

"Wh-what was that?" Aunt Tish's eyes had been shut tight so she wouldn't see the dangerous curves in the road. She had missed seeing the big car that had skimmed past them. Now all that remained was a thin haze of dust.

"A road hog!" Annette told her shakily. Then, as she began to recover from her fright, Annette became angry. "He almost crowded us over the edge! And I'm only hoping he didn't do it to Jinks and Lisa!"

She stepped on the gas and went to find out how they had made out. To her immense relief, they were safe—but as shaken as she had been.

Jinks's car was perched halfway up the banked edge of the road, over a straight two-hundred-foot drop, and they were still sitting in it, looking as if they were wondering what had happened.

Annette pulled ahead and stopped while Jinks carefully got back onto the road again.

"Wow! Is that how the locals drive in Arizona?" he teased Lisa. But his voice was a little shaky.

"I don't think he was anybody who lives in Pine Mesa. He'd have more sense than to drive that fast on our mountain roads if he knew them!" Lisa told him quickly.

Annette thought she might recognize that red-bearded man if she saw him again. There couldn't be many people with flaming red hair in the neighborhood. She would watch for him in Pine Mesa.

They went on again without any delay. The sun was dropping lower every minute and soon it would be gone.

They were on a fairly level road that wound among the tall, red sandstone cliffs and pinnacles of a high valley, when Jinks signaled a halt and then pulled off the road to wait for Annette and Aunt Tish.

"Something wrong?" Annette asked as she pulled up beside them.

Lisa pointed to a cloud of dust that had appeared on the road ahead. "Herd of sheep coming around the foot of that cliff. We'd better not try to get past them."

"Suits me," Annette said. "I'd like to stretch a little." She pulled off the road and got out.

As the flock of sheep came up, the friends saw that a small Navajo boy on a burro was the herder.

Annette expected Aunt Tish to exclaim over his picturesque appearance, but Aunt Tish was already busy sketching one of the distant pinnacles.

A tall, canvas-covered wagon came along after the sheep. It was heavily loaded with household goods, odds and ends of furniture, and bedding. Serious-looking Navajo women and youngsters peered out from the rear, but none of them answered Lisa's greeting.

Not knowing the Navajo customs, Jinks said, "Not very friendly, are they?"

"They are when they get to know you and trust you," Lisa told him. "Dad has some fine Navajo friends. They'd do anything for him."

"This must be the grandfather of the family." Annette nodded toward a solitary figure bringing up the rear of the procession, far enough behind to avoid the dust cloud from the wagon.

Lisa stared at the approaching figure, and Annette asked, "Why the funny look? Do you know him?"

"Thomas Yazzie! Wait!" Lisa called, as the Indian rode on past them.

At the sound of his name, the rider turned a bronzed face toward her in surprise. A moment later his serious face broke into a grin, and he wheeled his horse to ride over to her. "Miss Lisa! You come home. It is good!"

"But what are you doing here?" Lisa asked. And as Annette and Jinks stood staring up at him, Lisa explained hastily, "Thomas Yazzie is Dad's foreman on the remodeling job. He hires the Navajo workmen and supervises them for Dad."

The Navajo headman sat up straight with a

proud expression, thinking about his days as foreman. "Aou! Yes! Thomas Yazzie in charge." Then he sobered and shook his head gravely. And being more familiar with the Navajo language, Thomas Yazzie said in broken English, "But nobody work now, so no boss. I go to summer range with my family."

"Nobody working?" Lisa looked stunned. "Why not?"

"Very bad luck come. Mr. Kerry say no work for long time. You ask him. He tell you." He touched the brim of his tall felt hat, wheeled his mount, and rode on out after the wagon.

"Bad luck!" Lisa looked after him, dazed. "Oh, I want to get home as fast as I can!"

"Of course you do! We'll go right now. Jinks can wait for Aunt Tish!" Annette was already hurrying Lisa toward her car.

"Sure!" Jinks watched them get into the car and drive off, and then he settled down for another half-hour wait for Aunt Tish to get the shape of the pinnacle sketched exactly right.

"Now, don't worry, Lisa," Annette said, trying

THE DESERT INN MYSTERY 37

to comfort her friend. "At least Thomas Yazzie didn't say anything was wrong with your folks."

"No, he didn't." The thought seemed to cheer up Lisa for a moment, but as they sped along as fast as Annette felt was safe, Lisa looked worried again. "I'm glad we only have a couple of miles to go."

Annette tried to take Lisa's mind off her worrying. "Say, this *is* a pretty little valley. I never saw so many wildflowers, and so many varieties."

Lisa managed a smile. "They *are* pretty." She glanced at the long slope carpeted with rainbow colors. "And the mesquite trees up at the old silver mine are in full bloom."

"I'll have to bring Aunt Tish out to paint that view. It's terrific!" Annette said cheerfully.

"The Indians don't think so. They say the mine is taboo, even haunted. They won't go near it."

"For goodness' sake! What's the story?"

"I've heard all sorts of rumors, but Dad says that a little over twenty years ago, three men were trapped in there by a mysterious explosion. The tunnel collapsed and buried them." Lisa shuddered and so did Annette.

"Ugh! I'd hate to be a miner!" Annette cried.

"The strange part of it, Dad says, is that supposedly they weren't miners at all. People suspected they were bank robbers hiding from a Tucson holdup. Of course, if they were, they must have had the money with them, because it was never located. But Dad thinks the bank robber story was made up to make the accident sound more romantic. He believes the men were really tramps camping out there and trying to do some amateur mining. Dynamite's awfully dangerous if you don't know how to use it."

"Didn't they ever find the bodies?" Annette shivered.

Lisa shook her head. "A rescue team went up, but the shaft had collapsed and there was no chance of getting down to look for them."

"So the poor fellows, whoever they were, are still up there. No wonder people think the mine's haunted!"

Soon they were coming into Pine Mesa. Annette forgot the haunted mine in her admiration of the tall sycamores and feathery tamarisks that bordered the wide, quiet main street. It was a much larger town than she had expected to see.

Lisa smiled proudly. "We're the county seat, as well as the oldest settlement in the county. There's been a lot of history made here, though we *have* slowed down the last few years. But we're going to wake up again!

"That's our place!" Lisa pointed out a two-story house with the tall windows, wide porch, and steep front steps of early days. A neat white fence surrounded the green lawn, and brightly flowered acacia trees stood up tall and straight on either side of the walk.

"How pretty!" Annette brought her car to a stop. "Aunt Tish will be sure to want to paint it!"

"Wait till she sees the old stage station!" Lisa told her. "You can still see bullet holes in the adobe walls!"

A moment later, Lisa was out of the car. "Come on. Mom is probably back from her hospital duty. She'll be delighted to see you." She was smiling, but Annette could see how tense she was.

They hurried up the walk together and Lisa unlocked the door and flung it open. "Mom! I'm home!"

But there was no answer.

Lisa called, a little louder, "Marie!" and hurried down the long hall toward the closed kitchen door. She went in, calling, "Marie! Where are you?"

Annette waited in the front hall, which was dark and cool and smelled old and somehow a little musty, though the wood of the hat rack was polished, and the mirror that hung inside its pegs was spotless.

Lisa came out of the kitchen and hurried to her friend.

"Now *Marie's* gone! The kitchen is all slicked up. No signs of dinner getting cooked."

Annette could see that she was afraid again. "I bet your dad knows where they are. Where would he be this time of day?"

"Why, at the station, I guess!" Lisa looked relieved. "And that's just where Mom and Marie are, too!" She grabbed Annette's hand and pulled

her toward the door. "Come on! We'll walk in on them. They probably aren't expecting us yet!"

They ran down the walk, hand in hand like two small children, and got back into the car.

"We're only going one block, but we might as well go in style!" Lisa smiled as they started away from the curb.

It was actually less than a block to the station. The old buildings stood in a square surrounded by a high adobe wall broken in a couple of places. There was a main building which showed signs of having been repaired and painted recently. Its thirty-inch-deep window recesses framed wavy old glass that had stood up to fifty or sixty summers and winters since peace had come to the desert. But there were bullet holes in the walls alongside the narrow perpendicular slits that had served as windows in the days of "the Indian trouble."

The girls left the car at the curb and went inside. From somewhere inside the main building came the sound of hammering. But they heard no voices.

"It's spooky, isn't it, thinking about all those bullet holes?" Annette spoke in almost a whisper.

"Dad! It's me, Lisa!"

The hammering stopped, and a tall, sandy-haired man came hurrying out, hammer in hand. He dropped the tool when he saw Lisa and, smiling, held out his arms to her.

"Honey!"

Lisa ran to him and hugged him hard. "Dad! It's so good to see you. I was so worried!"

He lost his smile. "What did Mother tell you?"

"I haven't seen her yet." Lisa suddenly remembered her manners. She let go of her father and turned to Annette. "Annette, this is my dad! Dad, this is Annette, my very best friend!"

"Glad to see you, young lady. Mom and I have been reading about you for several months. My girl's letters talked about how smart and talented you are!"

Annette blushed in spite of herself and cast a reproachful look at Lisa, who was grinning proudly. "Why, thanks, Mr. Kerry."

"Just telling the truth, that's all." He turned to

Lisa. "I suppose Mother is still at the hospital helping Doc Marlow take care of Charley."

"Oh, is Charley sick? No wonder Marie wasn't at the house. She's probably nursing him, too."

"I imagine so." Lon Kerry sighed and looked gloomy. "She and little Theresa have hardly left his side since he's been at Doc's."

"You didn't say what was the matter with Charley," Lisa reminded her father.

Lon Kerry picked up the hammer and hung it on his belt. "I think I'd better show you. Come along, both of you."

He led them toward the rear of the walled square, past a small caretaker's house where, he explained, Charley and Marie Nez lived with their eight-year-old, Theresa. It was handy for them, with Charley at work on the station and Marie cooking for the Kerrys.

Then, as they came to the big half-adobe and half-wooden barn, he didn't have to explain what had happened inside it. The blackened adobe and the charred framework of the door told the story.

"When did it happen?" Lisa looked sick, and

Annette quickly slipped an arm around her waist.

"Night before last. Charley tried to put out the flames with buckets of water, but they had made too much headway by the time he discovered them."

"Was he hurt badly?" Lisa asked.

"His hands were scorched, but he'll be all right in another day or so," her father replied.

"I'm glad of that. How did the fire start, Dad?"

"All I know is that Charley saw the flames as he drove his wagon in about midnight. He and the family had been visiting relatives back home on the reservation. He sent Marie to call me, and I rounded up the volunteer fire department. But it moved too fast to be stopped." And he added grimly, "Whoever started it did a good job!"

"Started it?" Lisa was horrified at the thought. "Who would do such a thing?"

"I don't know. I wish I could find out. I didn't know there was anyone in Pine Mesa who hated us enough for that."

"But why would they do it?" Lisa wailed. "I thought everybody was so happy that you were fixing up this place to bring the tourist trade here and put Pine Mesa back on the map!"

"I thought so, too, Lisa," her father told her gravely, "but somebody doesn't want us to. Somebody who knew we had all the furniture for the inn stored in there, and that I'd have no chance of replacing it now."

"All those lovely old antiques Mother and you bought up—were they in there, too?"

"Every one. And the handmade pine tables and chairs that the Navajo carpenters had spent six months making!"

"Then—there's no chance now of opening this fall, I guess."

"Or next fall, for that matter," Lon Kerry said bitterly. "We can't even count on that, the way things are." "

CHAPTER 4

The Offer

If I could only do something to help! Annette thought unhappily as Lisa and her father stood staring hopelessly at the charred remains of the valuable furnishings. If she had had a lot of money . . . but she didn't, so there was no use "if-ing" about that.

Lon Kerry saw her expression when he turned. He spoke quickly, even managing a smile. "But right now we're going to forget about it and think about something a little more pleasant. Like that good dinner your mother's been planning for you girls, Lisa. And seeing some of your old friends again. I swear I've been pestered to death every day by some of them, wanting to know how soon you'd be here to visit us."

Lisa dashed away the last trace of a tear and smiled affectionately at her father. "Wait till they meet Annette! They'll forget they missed me!"

"Oh, I don't know!" Annette flashed a teasing look at her friend. "I could mention a certain someone who wouldn't agree with that! And he's probably just checking in right this minute at the hotel with our chaperone."

"What's this?" Lon Kerry's blue eyes twinkled as he saw the blush rise on his daughter's cheeks.

"Annette!" Lisa scolded her friend. "Don't say silly things! You know Jinks Bradley came to help his aunt find scenery to paint!"

"*Hmmph!*" Her father led them away from the burned barn. "Let's go meet the visitors and ask them to a good home-cooked meal, and you can settle the argument later."

They were locking the front gate of the old stage station a few minutes later when a late-model convertible, with plenty of chrome work, drew up behind Annette's Monster. It was a big car, one of the most expensive, but it was streaked with desert dust, just like the Monster.

Annette noticed the big car at once because she was unconsciously watching for the one that size that had almost run them over the canyon edge.

But the man at the wheel had no flaming red beard. This one was wearing a baseball-type cap with some sort of embroidered design on the front. Probably belongs to a swanky golf club, Annette thought as she sized him up at a glance. Not bad, if you like the type.

The young man slipped out of his car and sauntered over to them with a confident swagger. "Mr. Kerry?" he asked in a pleasant voice, flashing a little smile at Annette and Lisa in turn, as they stood a little apart.

"Yes?" Lon Kerry was tired and harassed.

"I'd like a few words with you, Mr. Kerry. It's on a rather important matter. My name is John Iverson, of San Diego. I know it doesn't mean anything to you at the moment, but I think you might be interested in my errand."

"Why—of course, Mr. Iverson. Just a moment." Kerry turned to the girls, both of whom were checking out the young man while they pretended to be interested in something across the street. "You girls go on to the hotel and deliver that invitation. I'll be along in a few minutes." He unlocked the gate and went inside with the stranger, and the girls went back to the car.

"Probably a salesman," Lisa said with a sigh as she settled down.

"With a wife and six kids in San Diego!" Annette added jokingly.

Cheerful Mrs. Kerry was busy in her kitchen, with Marie and little Theresa, when the girls came in from their errand at the hotel across the street.

The bulletin about Charley Nez was encouraging. Doc Marlow was letting Marie take him home tonight to the station because his burns were healing so well.

"So this is a celebration for all of us," Mrs. Kerry told the girls. "What if we can't open the inn this fall? Next year we'll be on our feet again and going strong!"

Later, when Annette went over to the hotel and brought Aunt Tish and Jinks back with her to dinner, she was delighted to see Aunt Tish and Mrs. Kerry hit it off at once like old friends.

Marie even managed a smile when Aunt Tish took over in the kitchen to show Mrs. Kerry and her a shortcut with the biscuits.

But when the early dinner hour came, there was still no sign of Mr. Kerry.

"That salesman must have had something terrific to try to sell Dad!" Lisa and Annette were sitting in the old rockers on the front porch, watching for Mr. Kerry.

Jinks, slicked up and very happy, sat on the steps at their feet. "Maybe we ought to walk up there and break up the conference," Jinks suggested. The smell of roasting meat was in the air, and he was as hollow as usual.

Annette stopped rocking and started to get up. But as she moved, she caught Jinks's eye. If ever a look said, "Remember, three's a crowd!"

Jinks's did. She settled back in the rocker. "Run along, kiddies! I'm too exhausted."

But Jinks didn't get his walk with Lisa after all. They had reached the front gate when Lisa said, "Why, here comes Dad now!" She ran out to meet her father as he came along the tree-shaded sidewalk, deep in conversation with John Iverson. Jinks hesitated a moment, then walked back to the porch and Annette.

Outside the gate, Mr. Kerry was introducing Iverson to Lisa, and Iverson was holding her hand as he paid her some sort of a compliment that made her smile and look shy. Neither Annette nor Jinks missed it.

Annette teased Jinks, "Hmm! Looks like a city slicker to me!" But Jinks didn't answer, and Annette felt sorry she had tried to tease him when she saw his long face. Clearly, Jinks had already made up his mind that he would have a rival.

After a minute or two, Iverson went across the street to the hotel, and Mr. Kerry walked slowly up the path with Lisa.

As they came close enough for Annette to see

their expressions, she saw that something serious was in the wind. Then she heard Lisa say, "I'm glad you said no, Dad."

"But I didn't," Lon Kerry gravely told his daughter. "I said I would think it over and let him know as soon as possible. I may not be able to refuse."

Then they were at the foot of the steps, and Lisa was introducing Jinks to her father. She seemed very subdued.

I hope nothing more has happened, Annette thought. The fire was bad enough.

Mr. Kerry seemed glad to meet Jinks and later, in the house, to welcome Aunt Tish to Pine Mesa. But it was plain to Annette that all three of the Kerrys were covering up some deep worry to be pleasant to their dinner guests.

Aunt Tish was thoroughly charmed with the old house. She raved about the antique furniture, the family possessions that had been brought overland in the 1870s, the priceless bits and pieces of the past that Lon Kerry had dreamed of re-creating at the inn.

"And we have an attic full of more of them,

more than we'll ever need to furnish the inn."
Mrs. Kerry told her.

"I'd like to browse around up there!" Aunt
Tish exclaimed. "May I—tomorrow? If there's
anything I adore, it's antiques!"

"I'll give you a big apron and a dust cap and
turn you loose up there tomorrow after church.
How'll that be?" Mrs. Kerry smiled.

"Perfect! And Jinks can come along with me
and scare away the spiders, if there are any!"

"You'll find plenty of them!" Mr. Kerry
assured her. "Nothing up there has been moved for
twenty-five years."

So it was arranged. And it was only a short time
after dinner that Aunt Tish admitted that she was
ready for a good night's rest after the long trip.

Jinks would have liked to do a little resting on
the porch steps in the moonlight, but he wasn't
too disappointed when Mrs. Kerry firmly
announced that the girls were going to get their
rest early, too. There was a long week ahead and
they would probably be very busy, once Lisa's
old friends heard she was back.

Though Annette and Lisa tumbled into their twin beds in Lisa's room promptly and called, "Good night!" to each other, they didn't sleep at once.

Lisa had had a long talk downstairs with her parents while Annette was getting ready for bed. When she had come upstairs, she had tried to be cheerful. It hadn't deceived her friend. I can't ask her what's going on, Annette had thought. She'll tell me soon.

But Lisa didn't. And a long time after they had lain silent in their beds, Annette was sure that she heard a small sob from Lisa.

When it came a second time, she knew she hadn't been mistaken. She sat up, clasping her knees, and addressed the adjacent bed. "You might as well tell me what's happened, Lisa. If you don't, neither of us is going to get a smidgen of sleep tonight."

"Oh, Annette!" Lisa sat up abruptly. "I'm sorry. I didn't mean to keep you awake. But Dad and Mom are thinking of selling the stage station!" She was crying now. "After all Dad's wonderful plans! It doesn't seem fair."

"But—if he gets a good price, he can remodel some other old place into an inn, can't he?" Annette took a practical view.

"That's just the point. Mr. Iverson says he can only pay about half of what Dad has invested already in the station. He says he hasn't any more to spend. And Dad is afraid he'll have to take it, or be left with a useless bunch of buildings and not even enough money to pay taxes on them!"

"Huh! Sounds like Iverson's looking for a bargain!" Annette hadn't liked him from the start. "He's driving around in a pretty swell car if he's short of money."

"Dad says he rented it or it belongs to some friend, or something. Dad likes him. He says he'd rather sell it to someone like Mr. Iverson, who wants it for sentimental reasons, than to give it back to the bank that sold it to him."

"Sentimental reasons?" Annette snorted. "I bet he's buying it for some building company that wants to use your dad's ideas and make an inn!"

"No, really! Mr. Iverson says his grandfather was the first division agent at the station when the stage line was established. He wants to live at the station and settle down here, he told Dad."

"Oh." Annette had no reason to doubt John Iverson's story. Only it was too bad he couldn't offer a more reasonable price for the place. "Well, I hope your dad thinks of some way to hold onto the station."

"He and Mom are trying, but it looks hopeless."

"Don't give up yet, Lisa. Don't forget how sunk we were about this trip, and how all of a sudden it worked out right for us to come!"

"It did, didn't it?" Lisa sounded almost cheerful, remembering. "Maybe this will, too!"

"Sure it will!" Annette wriggled down under the covers with a yawn. "You'll see!"

Soon both tired girls were asleep.

But there were others in Pine Mesa who were wide-awake. One was John Iverson. And the other was the man with the flaming red hair who had made a round-trip to Flagstaff to pick him up that day—the same red-bearded man who had almost crowded Annette's car off the mountain road.

CHAPTER 5

A Live Ghost

The shack where Gold-Tooth Shay was waiting
for John Iverson was in a run-down neighborhood beyond the end of the street. Next door, a
noisy barroom featured a jukebox that blared day
and night. Each time the barroom door opened
for someone to enter or leave, the sound of shuf-
fling feet, laughter, and the clink of glasses min-
gled with the jukebox racket made the big man
restless and resentful.

It was well onto midnight, and Iverson hadn't
shown up yet.

"Him livin' in a swell hotel, and me stuck in
this hole!" he muttered to himself. "I'm as big a

59

pardner in this as he is. I'm sick of playin' second fiddle, and tired of hidin' behind all these whiskers. Got a good mind to shave 'em off." He went over to glower at himself in the cheap mirror over the grimy washbasin. He pulled the whiskers aside and smiled at himself, showing the gold tooth in all its gleaming splendor. Then he reached for the razor lying beside the basin and tested its blade with his thumb.

The door behind him had opened, and John Iverson stood watching him with a cynical expression. "Better not, Shay. Leave them on a couple of days more. Then you can shave."

"Huh?" The big man looked sheepish as he hastily put the razor down and turned his back to the mirror. "So you got here."

"I had to wait till the town went to sleep." Iverson smiled and ignored his partner's scowl.

"How did you make out with Kerry? Do we get the station?"

"Very soon. He's stalling for time, but it won't do him any good. I've made inquiries around town. He's in too deep to raise any money to go on with the remodeling."

"I guess that fire of mine did the trick, hey?"

"Right! You did a good job!"

"Guess I get some good ideas now an' then, don't I?" Shay grinned again.

"Just don't get one to clip off that beard. That tooth of yours is a dead giveaway," Iverson told him coolly.

"But the Indian's the only guy I've seen around that I remember from the old days. And he's in the hospital. There's nobody'd recognize me."

"You can't be sure. And we can't take chances. There's too much in it." Iverson's voice cracked like a whip, and his eyes were cold as he faced the childlike big man.

"Okay, okay, I'll keep the whiskers."

"That's the stuff!" Iverson laughed. There was no use quarreling now. They needed each other. "You don't like the whiskers, and I don't like being cooped up in this dead burg. But we'll both be on our way in a couple of days."

"Sure, John." Shay nodded. "What's next?"

"Keep out of sight. Those two girls you nearly ran off the road this afternoon are Kerry's daughter and a school friend. They'd be bound to spot you and they might try to make trouble for you."

"They better not!" The snarl on Shay's face wiped off all traces of an easy good nature. He looked mean and dangerous.

"We might save ourselves a little time later on," Iverson suggested quickly. "With Charley Nez still in the hospital and his old woman and kid sleeping at the Kerry place, there's nobody around the station tonight. We can start looking for the stuff right now. What do you say?"

Shay hesitated. The sound of the jukebox music and the laughter of the dancers were loud in the room. He had been thinking of going next door as soon as Iverson left. He met Iverson's eyes and saw that Iverson had read his mind.

"Okay," he agreed sullenly. "Maybe we'll come up lucky and find it tonight. I sure didn't turn up any signs of it night before last when I was prowlin' around before the fire."

John Iverson took a much-folded letter from his inner coat pocket and studied it, frowning. "If my old man had just come right out and said where to look, we'd have it easier. All he wrote was 'tunnel to the creek.' You sure you didn't miss seeing a trapdoor on the barn floor or the main building somewhere? Maybe a door in one of the walls?"

"Nope. I told you that half a dozen times."

"Then there's some other way to get into some kind of a tunnel. The letter says so, and Pa was dying when he wrote it. He wouldn't fool around."

"Don't seem likely. My letter said the same thing. And the letter Baxter's widow got. Our money's hid in an old nail keg in a tunnel at the station."

"I used to wonder what happened to that money when I was growing up, but every time I went to see Pa in State Prison, the guard kept too close for me to ask." John Iverson grinned. "Well, we've just about caught up with it now.

"I never did hear how Pa happened to be carrying the whole fifty thousand when you blew up the mine and scattered. Why didn't you just divvy up all the money right then?"

"Your pa was running things. He wanted us to check in for another bank job at Vegas, so he held off the split. We waited up there, but he didn't show up. Later on, we read where he'd tried a bank holdup at Flagstaff and had been caught. They never did tie him up with the Tucson job. And we never heard any more about him till he managed to get those three letters mailed outside the prison, just before he died."

"Well, you'll get your split pretty soon now."

"Yeah!" The big man licked his lips.

"Come on, we've still got a few hours before daylight to look around in there while the place is empty," Iverson said.

A few minutes later, they were in the narrow alley at the rear of the station. The heavy wooden gate was bolted.

"I can climb it easy and open it. Wouldn't want you to get your elegant clothes mussed up." Shay grinned.

"No need to climb. There's a break in the wall

in back of the caretaker's house. I saw it today. We can slip through easily."

The break wasn't wide enough for Shay, so he worked a chunk of adobe brick loose to enlarge it—and accidentally dropped a heavy piece to the cemented ground.

A few feet away, on the screened back porch, Marie had made up a bed for her recovering husband in the cool air. Now Charley sat up suddenly, staring suspiciously into the darkness.

Something bulky was moving toward him in the shadow of the old acacia tree. He could see what looked like the figure of a man. He flashed his light on it. "Who is that?"

A huge man, bearded and shaggy-haired, stopped a few feet away, glaring at Charley with eyes enormous in the blinding flashlight. His lips drew back in a snarl of surprise and showed a big gold tooth gleaming in the center of his mouth.

"*Ai!*" Charley dropped the flashlight in terror. "*Ai!* Marie! Come quick! A ghost!"

And when Marie and Theresa came stumbling in to see what was going on, Charley was under the bedcovers, shaking with fear.

The two intruders were at the end of the alley by then and moving fast. "Get back to the shack and stay there till you hear from me," Iverson snapped. And as Shay melted into the darkness, Iverson hurried to the back door of the hotel.

He had left the door unlocked earlier when he had slipped out without being seen. To his relief, it was still unlocked. He ran swiftly up the back stairs to his room.

It was a few minutes later that Sheriff Martinez woke Lon Kerry to tell him, "The Nez family dragged me out of bed. They're scared stiff."

Lon Kerry looked grim. "The firebug again?"

"If it was, he didn't get a chance to do his dirty work. Charley saw him in time and yelled blue murder. Funny part is, Charley claims it was a ghost!"

"A ghost?" Kerry thought he hadn't heard right.

"Yep! Charley got a close look, and he's still shaking. Claims it was one of those three strangers who blew themselves to kingdom come in the old silver mine twenty years ago.

One of them had a big gold tooth in the front of his mouth. Called himself Gold-Tooth Shay. Charley says this was him—that is, his ghost!"

Kerry hurried into an overcoat as the sheriff continued. "I found footprints by that hole in the wall. It was probably some tramp looking for a place to sleep."

"Or that firebug, come back to finish the job!" Kerry said bitterly as they started down the street toward the station. "Guess he thinks he hasn't done enough to us!"

Lon Kerry and the sheriff had been friends for many years, and the sheriff shared the town's indignation over the fire. "I can't figure why anybody'd try to stop you from giving the town a boost with your inn!"

"Well, whoever did it made a good job of it, Tim. I'm licked. I don't know where to turn."

John Iverson watched them from his hotel window as they disappeared in the direction of the station. And he was waiting near his open window when they came back a few minutes later. In the still night air, the sheriff's voice boomed, "—still thinks it was the ghost of Gold-Tooth Shay, so I guess it's no use trying to talk him out of it."

"—such nonsense." Kerry's voice was softer but became quite distinct to Iverson's ears. "But it shouldn't be hard to locate that tramp."

"Don't worry, Lon. I'll have the boys comb the alleys and the rooming houses for him tomorrow, Sunday or not. We'll ask him some questions about that fire of yours when we find him, too."

Iverson scowled. He would have to go back to Shay's shack again and warn him to find a safer hiding place. He knew Shay wouldn't go far, with the bank loot practically theirs now.

The answer seemed to be the "haunted" mine itself. Nobody would think of looking for him there, and he could join Iverson quickly once Kerry had signed over the station in return for Iverson's check. They would have to move fast, before the phony check could get to the San Diego bank on which Iverson planned to draw it.

* * *

"I'll be glad when we kick the dust of this dead hole off our boots," Shay said with a growl as he set out in the chilly dawn for the mine.

"It won't be long now," Iverson assured him smugly. "We've got Kerry over a barrel."

But Iverson wasn't quite right about that!

Annette was sitting up in bed, in the dark, at that very moment, trying to think up some way to help the Kerrys out of their fix. And her brown eyes were suddenly wide open as an idea came to her.

"Lisa!" She leaned over and shook her friend in the other twin bed. "Listen to this! I've got a wonderful idea!"

And Lisa, suddenly wide-awake, too, listened while Annette rattled off her sudden inspiration. When she stopped to catch her breath, Lisa added a few touches to the idea. And before they knew it, they were giggling and laughing happily over the whole thing.

In the Kerrys' room down the hall, Lisa's parents were wide-awake, too. Her father was pacing the floor.

"I'll go to the bank once more on Monday,"

Mr. Kerry was saying grimly, "but I'm afraid it won't do any good. We're licked."

For once, Mrs. Kerry's happy spirits disappeared. She was nodding slowly in agreement with her husband's words. There didn't seem to be anything to say.

"Did you hear that?" Mr. Kerry asked suddenly.

She looked startled as she listened. Unmistakable sounds of laughter were coming from Lisa's room down the hall. Then they heard the door open and the sound of slippered footsteps in the hallway.

"Mom! Dad! Wake up! Annette has just had a terrific idea! Can we come in and tell you?"

Mrs. Kerry was lighting the lamp at her bedside. "Come in!"

They burst in, still giggling, and Lisa turned to Annette. "Tell them yourself!"

But Annette was suddenly shy. It was one thing telling her idea to her friend, and another telling it to these grave-faced, worried elders. "No, you tell."

And Lisa, excitedly, did. "It's those things up

in the attic. All those lovely things from Grandpa Newsome's house, Mom. And lots of our own stuff out in the barn, stuff we never use. We've got lots more than we'd need to open an antiques shop in the station. And then we could raise enough money to open the inn!"

"Antiques shop!" Her father looked stunned for a moment. "But—" Lon Kerry frowned.

Mrs. Kerry interrupted. "Annette! That's it!" She bounced back into her usual cheerful mood in a flash. "We can tidy up the station in a couple of days!"

"And Aunt Tish can paint some posters advertising the shop!" Annette added.

"And there are plenty of the kids home on vacation who can help cart the stuff down from the attic and over to the station for us!"

They were still planning happily long after John Iverson, across the street in the hotel, had fallen asleep with happy thoughts of the search he would make, along about day after tomorrow, when Lon Kerry had signed over the property to him for a worthless check.

CHAPTER 6

The Project

The more the Kerrys considered Annette's suggestion of opening an antiques shop in the station, the better they thought it sounded. And though Annette and Lisa slept well the rest of the night, Lisa's parents were still discussing ways and means when the Sunday morning sun rose.

Later, while Lisa and Annette were meeting Lisa's old school friends after church, Lon Kerry mentioned the plan to Sheriff Martinez and asked his advice.

"Sounds great," the sheriff admitted cautiously, "but it seems to me you'll need some cash, as well as the things you're planning to sell. The old place is pretty rickety. And I noticed the roof is just about gone in a couple of places. That'll take some investment, Lon."

"I'm figuring on that," Kerry told him. "I'll talk to the bank folks tomorrow. I'm pretty sure I can get a thousand dollars more on the mortgage, once they hear our plans."

"Sure hope so, Lon. I'd like to see you have some good luck for a change!"

"Don't forget, we're having company for Sunday dinner." Mrs. Kerry laid her hand on her husband's arm. And they gathered the girls from a chattering group of Lisa's friends and went home to meet Aunt Tish and her nephew and tell them about the new project.

Aunt Tish had already arrived and was poking around in the dimness of the attic, with Jinks holding a flashlight and armed with a broom to dispose of any spiders daring enough to confront Aunt Tish.

Annette and Lisa ran up to tell them what was being planned for the contents of the attic.

"All this lovely stuff—sold?" Aunt Tish clasped

her hands around a Wedgwood vase that had held Grandma Newsome's roses seventy years ago. "Oh, no!" She was sitting on the dusty floor, surrounded by the contents of an ancient trunk.

"It isn't doing any good here," Annette told her. "And Lisa's folks don't mind parting with it."

"Indeed not!" Lisa agreed happily. "Dad's often wondered what would happen to it. He knows I'm going to have everything up to date in *my* house—when I have one!"

"Hmph!" Aunt Tish patted the vase. "Young people!" And she asked, frowning, "When you get the place all stocked with these priceless things, suppose no one comes to buy them?"

"But they will!" Annette was positive. "We'll get someone to paint posters and we'll ride around and stick them on fence posts and telephone poles—you know. And if the poster is cute enough, lots of people will come. And if they come, they'll buy!" Annette stole a quick look at Aunt Tish's face and then she sighed audibly. "Of course, we have to find somebody who can paint just the right kind of poster. I mean—" She stole another look at Jinks's aunt to see how she was taking the hint.

Aunt Tish put the Wedgwood vase down tenderly and got to her feet with a grunt. "I know what you mean. And I'll paint your poster."

"Hooray for Aunt Tish!" Jinks beamed through his thick lenses and gave Aunt Tish a hug.

Aunt Tish pushed him away abruptly and tried to look severe. "And next time you want something"—she wagged a finger at Annette—"come out and ask for it! Now, why don't we go take a look at the station and see what work it's going to take to make it over into an antiques shop?"

But Mr. and Mrs. Kerry insisted on dinner first and inspection afterward. It was a merry meal and everyone's spirits were high.

Across the street at the hotel, John Iverson had slept late after his midnight adventure with Gold-Tooth Shay. He was lazily reading the Sunday paper near his front-room window when he heard voices and laughter in the Kerry house.

He was puzzled. He hadn't expected the Kerrys to be in a very cheerful mood today. What could have happened to change their outlook?

A few minutes later, he was surprised to see the Kerrys and their guest, Annette, come out, followed by the Bradley woman and her nephew. They were all chatting cheerfully as they came down the path.

Now, they were walking, two by two, up the street toward the station, and Lon Kerry was smiling.

Suddenly, Iverson threw aside the paper and began to dress quickly. He hadn't intended to see Lon Kerry today. He had planned to wait till tomorrow. But it was evident that something had happened to cheer Kerry up. He had to find out what it was.

As Mr. Kerry opened the windows and doors, Annette could see that the paint was peeling off the walls and that daylight was coming through the roof in a couple of places. She hoped it didn't look as discouraging to the others as it did to her!

But the Kerrys didn't seem worried. Mr. Kerry showed them the holes in the roof and told them, "Last month's windstorm tore off a few tiles, but it won't take much to have them replaced. I'll have money for that in a few days—I hope." He smiled cheerfully. "And for a couple of other repairs."

He and Thomas Yazzie's Navajo workers had almost finished remodeling one wing.

"We'll keep this part shut off for the time being. The big room will do for the shop."

"When it's cleaned up!" Mrs. Kerry gave the girls a significant look, which they didn't miss.

Annette made believe she was feeling her arm muscle as she grinned. "What time does the bucket-and-mop squad report for duty?"

"Right after breakfast tomorrow. And don't eat too much or you might not be able to keep up with the rest of us!" Jinks teased.

"We talked to some of the kids at church," Lisa told her father, "and they all want to help if you'll let them." She threw a mischievous look at Annette. "I think Annette smiled at Jim and Dave and Billy Joe. They certainly fell all over themselves, offering!"

"Well, whoever's to blame, they're welcome!"

Lon Kerry laughed. "We need all the hands we can get to put this over!"

"I hope I'm not intruding—" John Iverson had come in quietly and was smiling at them from the doorway.

"Not in the least!" Lon Kerry told him cordially. "I meant to come by the hotel later to tell you that I've decided not to consider selling now."

John Iverson had heard enough snatches of conversation to know that some project was underway. It had been a blow that was taking all his willpower to conceal. "I'm sorry to hear that," he said with a wry smile. "I've been counting on living here."

"*Living* here?" Aunt Tish put her hands on her hips and stared at him. "Why here?" she asked bluntly.

"Why"—he smiled easily at Aunt Tish— "I suppose because I'm a sentimental type. As I explained to Mr. Kerry, my great-grandfather was the agent here years ago." There was a coldness behind his smile.

"And you almost persuaded me to sell it to

you." Kerry interrupted with a smile. "If it hadn't been for Annette here coming up with a solution, you'd have had it Monday!"

John Iverson glanced at Annette, a smile still on his face. "A pretty girl who's clever, too!" He spoke lightly.

But Annette, meeting his eyes, saw again the cold, hard look that he had given Aunt Tish. And in spite of herself, she looked away hastily and felt a shiver run down her spine.

"Indeed she is!" Lon Kerry laughed, and went on to tell Iverson their plans for opening an antiques shop.

"You are a gambler at heart, Mr. Kerry." Iverson smiled thinly. "I wish you luck."

Annette thought wryly, But what kind of luck? And as she went to look for Mrs. Kerry and Aunt Tish, who had gone out into the courtyard, she tried to think what it was that Iverson's cold, hard eyes had reminded her of.

It wasn't till she was out in the sunshine, where the two ladies were talking to Marie beside the fountain, that she remembered. It was the eyes of a rattlesnake that had stared back at her through the glass pane in the reptile house of the zoo. Iverson's eyes were of the same pale color and coldness!

Now I'm being dramatic! she told herself. He's probably a character who doesn't like not getting his own way. Or else he just doesn't like girls!

But a few minutes later, she was ready to take back the second half of that guess—at least so far as Lisa was concerned. For he came strolling out with her, and she was listening with a smile as he gestured comically to illustrate some yarn he apparently was telling to amuse her. They both laughed as he finished.

And behind them, quite a way behind them, in fact, Mr. Kerry and Jinks came out into the sunshine, arm in arm, as Kerry pointed out various things around the place that he intended to fix up. Jinks was trying to look interested, but his eyes were following Lisa and the tall, good-looking Iverson as they moved away together.

Poor Jinks! It must be awful to be so in love! Annette thought. But there wasn't a thing she could

do to help him, so she joined the ladies as they told
Marie what was going to happen to the station.

"It is good!" Marie nodded vigorously. "And if
the ghost comes again, this time we will be ready
for him. My man sleeps with a rifle beside the bed."

"Gracious, Marie! That's dangerous! It might
fall and go off and hit someone!" Mrs. Kerry
cried.

There was a small chuckle from somewhere
behind Annette, and when she turned to see
where it came from, she saw little Theresa. But
Theresa wasn't in her school outfit, a plain little
print dress. She had donned the velveteen blouse
and full long skirt of contrasting vivid colors that
the Navajo women they had seen on the reservation yesterday had been wearing. Her long black
hair was tied back with white wool spun yarn,
and she wore Navajo moccasins. She was carrying a young lamb named Esteban in her arms.

"Hi, cutie! My, how nice you look! I wish I
had my camera along!" Annette knelt down to
Theresa's level. "What are you chuckling about?"

Theresa leaned close with some difficulty,

because of the struggling baby lamb. She put her lips next to Annette's ear. "The gun is not loaded. It is one big bluff."

Annette whispered in return. "Don't tell anybody. I'll keep your secret!" And they laughed heartily together.

"There's my poster subject!" Aunt Tish was pointing dramatically at Theresa. "Against the fountain, the lamb at her feet. Wonderful! Jinks!" She looked around for Jinks. "Run, get my paints and my easel!"

Jinks looked uncertain. Mr. Kerry glowered a moment at being interrupted, then saw the reason. "Go on, lad! We can talk later." And as Jinks reluctantly started out toward the entrance, Kerry strode over to where Iverson was entertaining Lisa in a corner of the courtyard where there was a stone bench just big enough to hold two people, rather close together.

John Iverson rose at once, glancing at his watch. "I'm afraid I must run along. Didn't realize it was so late." He divided his smile between Lon Kerry and Lisa. "The charming company, of course!" Lisa blushed in response, and her father looked pleased.

Moments later, Iverson was on his way out, with a last wave to the rest of the group.

"Dad, Mr. Iverson is the nicest person. Do you know what he's going to do?" Lisa asked.

"Can't imagine, unless it's to head back to San Diego now that the place isn't for sale!" Mr. Kerry felt jovial.

Annette and Theresa had come over to show the lamb and the costume to them. She heard Lisa say, "He's such a good sport! He'll be around the rest of the week, anyhow, and he says he'll come over here every day and do anything he can to help us get ready to open! Isn't that the most unselfish thing you ever heard of?"

"Well, it's unusual. But maybe he finds the air—or something else around here—easy to take," her father teased, winking at Annette.

But Annette didn't feel very happy about having Iverson underfoot every day. And she knew Jinks wouldn't, either!

CHAPTER 7

Helping Hands

It was very quiet in the shadows of the vine-covered front porch of the Kerry house as the two girls swung slowly in the glider, each in her own corner, curled up against the pillows with one foot under her and one free for pushing. It had been quite a few minutes since either had broken the comfortable silence.

The town had gone to sleep an hour ago at least. Even the lights in the hotel across the way had been put out except for the night-light burning dimly over the desk in the lobby.

Somewhere inside the house a clock struck.

"Nine—ten—eleven—" Annette counted,

yawning. "Twelve o'clock. I hate to move—it's so pretty out here in the moonlight, and the honeysuckle smells so sweet—but we have a big day tomorrow!"

"We certainly have!" Lisa agreed, uncurling herself. "Billy Joe and Jim have promised to start painting, and Jinks is going to help Dad put up some shelves." Lisa smiled. "I suppose Mr. Iverson will be around to help, too. He's nice, isn't he?"

Annette stood up, stretching. "I guess so. Or maybe he still hopes he can talk your dad into selling if he hangs around."

Lisa frowned. "Why don't you like him, 'Nette?"

"Oh, I don't know. I suppose it's because he looks like a smoothie to me."

"Why, you hardly spoke to him. Where did you get such an idea?" Lisa asked.

"Oh"—Annette really had nothing to base her feelings on—"it's just a notion. You know how it is. People remind you of somebody, or something, you don't like, and right off you get the two mixed up in your mind. I guess that's all it is."

Lisa nodded. "I've done that myself lots of times. I remember one teacher—" She broke off suddenly and leaned forward to stare. "Isn't that Mr. Iverson going by?"

Annette studied the figure that rode briskly down the center of the moonlit street without a glance at the shadowy porch. "So it is! Wonder where he's been."

"Enjoying the moonlight, just the way we've been doing." Lisa sounded a little on the defensive.

The rider had turned in at the stable down the street by now, but Lisa still stood, watching.

"Wonder why he didn't go in that oversized car of his." Annette yawned again and linked her arm in Lisa's. "Come on, you'll see him tomorrow. Let's not wait."

"I wasn't waiting," Lisa protested. Annette could almost see the blush in spite of the darkness.

"He'll tell you all about it in the morning, dearie. How he thought about you and all that!" Annette grinned, pulling Lisa inside with her and closing the door firmly behind them.

But John Iverson had no intention of mentioning his moonlight ride to Lisa or anyone else. He had been out to the old mine to tell his partner that they might not get possession of the station as soon as they had hoped.

"But I'll have plenty of chances to look around for the tunnel, while I help the Kerrys and their friends," he had assured Gold-Tooth Shay.

"Yeah—but if you find it, how do we get to look for the keg without them knowin' it?" Shay had growled.

"I'll work that out. Just you sit tight up here and wait to hear from me. Don't let anybody see you."

"Okay! But I don't like this spooky place, anyhow."

"Maybe you'd rather be in jail. That's where you'll land if Charley Nez sees you again and calls the sheriff!" Iverson snapped.

So Shay had agreed to wait, for a few days at least. Maybe when the Kerrys' visitors had gone back to the Coast, Iverson would have a better chance to look for the hidden entrance of the tunnel. Meanwhile, he would play along.

* * *

Monday morning was bright and clear. Lisa, tip-toeing over to raise the window shades, blinked in surprise to see that the clock on her dresser said nine o'clock.

She let the nearest shade roll up with a bang that brought Annette upright in bed, looking star-tled and worried. "What happened?"

"We overslept!" Lisa laughed. Then, as she glanced out the open window toward the gate, she gave a gasp. "Look, Annette!"

Annette swung out of bed and staggered over, still half asleep. And as she peered down over Lisa's shoulder she laughed, too.

Lined up along the small white fence, Billy Joe, Jim, Dave, Karen, and Janey—all Lisa's friends, whom Annette had met yesterday at church—were waiting.

Each of them was dressed in his or her own idea of what a hard-working house cleaner or painter should wear. The girls had big aprons over their shorts and blouses, and their hair done up in color-ful scarfs tied with big rabbit-ear bows on top. They were armed with brooms, brushes, and pails.

The boys were in denims and gingham shirts, barefoot and wearing wide-brimmed "hayseed" straw hats. They carried all sorts of cleanup tools — buckets, paintbrushes, rakes, hoes, and shovels.

Dave heard the giggles up at the front window and waved to the girls. "Hi, sleepyheads! Did you say nine o'clock or noon?"

"We're sorry! Be with you in two shakes!" Lisa called down and retreated with Annette.

"Okay!" Jim shouted. Then he shouldered the rake and started whistling a work song. Everyone fell into line, laughing, and as Jim led the way up the middle of the street, the others joined in the whistling, more or less in tune.

"Wasn't that cute?" Lisa smiled as she and Annette hurried into work clothes.

"They're a lot of dolls!" Annette agreed. But she took a quick look out the window toward the hotel. There was no sign of Jinks. She thought with a sigh, Too bad Jinks couldn't have been in on that. Lisa would have liked it. But I suppose Aunt Tish isn't ready to leave yet, and he has to wait for her.

But a little later, when she and Lisa arrived at

the station, they found that Aunt Tish and Jinks had joined Mr. Kerry even earlier than the others.

Aunt Tish was busy sketching Theresa and her lamb in the sunny courtyard, and Jinks was nailing up a shelf that was to be painted along with the walls. There was a lot of kidding and laughter going on among the boys and girls, but the girls were doing a good job sweeping and mopping the big room, while the boys had already started painting one wall.

Mr. Kerry, looking cheerful, was superintending the whole job.

Annette and Lisa started on a window, one washing inside, the other outside, making funny faces at each other as they cleaned each ancient pane.

Janey came up to Annette, outside, while Lisa was getting clean water from the kitchen. "Got to talk fast before she gets back," she said. "Did you know that tomorrow's Lisa's birthday?"

Annette looked stricken. "Gosh, I forgot!"

"We're cooking up a surprise for her." Janey kept an eye toward the kitchen.

"Count Jinks and me in on it, whatever it is," Annette told her promptly. "What do you have in mind?"

"Well, her dad says if the boys get the painting done in the big room today, it has to set till Wednesday before it'll be dry enough for the second coat. That leaves us with nothing to do tomorrow, so we're going to surprise Lisa with a birthday picnic out somewhere. Maybe near the old mine."

"She'll love it," Annette agreed. "But—what about presents?"

"None of us are very rich right now, so we decided to pass up any presents and settle for the picnic instead. Mrs. Kerry's in on it. She's baking a cake this afternoon, and we'll sneak it out with us tomorrow."

Annette nodded and winked as Lisa started back with the pail of clean water. Janey slipped away back to her own job of sweeping the courtyard.

"What were you two buzzing about?" Lisa asked through the window.

"Oh, we were wondering what to do with ourselves tomorrow. Janey thought a picnic might be nice."

Lisa liked the idea. Annette could see that. And when Mrs. Kerry and Marie came from the house with lunch for all of them, everyone talked happily about tomorrow's picnic—but nobody mentioned that it was a birthday party.

Aunt Tish was in on it, too. She told Lisa, "I'll be finished with this poster tonight, and I'll come along on the picnic. I want to paint Theresa and her lamb against a real desert background, for the second poster."

Annette noticed that Lisa had been glancing often toward the front entrance. She guessed that her friend was hoping John Iverson would come to help as he had promised.

But they had almost finished their lunch before he arrived. He was with Mr. Kerry, who had left for the bank just before lunch.

Annette could see from Mr. Kerry's face that he had had a disappointment at the bank. He took Mrs. Kerry aside to tell her something, and when

she rejoined the others she looked worried, too.

But John Iverson was even more cheerful than he had been yesterday. In spite of his smart clothes, he whipped off his coat and got to work with a paintbrush, right along with the others.

And though the three local boys weren't pleased, they took his brisk suggestions about where and how to put on the paint. Jinks was the only one who sulked, but John Iverson ignored it good-naturedly. Even when Jinks accidentally kicked over a small can of paint that spattered Iverson's expensive shoes and stained his trouser cuffs, the older man seemed undisturbed.

"I'll be glad to pay for the cleaning, Mr. Iverson," Jinks insisted.

But Iverson laughed. "Forget it, sonny. Anybody can have an accident." He might have been speaking to a small boy, and Jinks's face turned red.

Lisa hurried to bring some rags and paint remover, and Jinks scrubbed hard for the next ten minutes to clean the floor.

Annette could see that he was miserable. And

when Lisa strolled out into the courtyard with John Iverson a few minutes later, when he had finished his part of the painting, Annette stopped to help Jinks.

"Never mind, I can do it by myself," he told her crossly. But she knew his crossness was with himself for his blundering. He had looked awkward and childish to Lisa in contrast to the self-possessed Iverson.

"Don't let him worry you," Annette told him impulsively. "Lisa likes you a lot. She's just being polite to him."

But Jinks scrubbed the floor harder and didn't look at her. *She* knew that *he* knew that *she* knew Lisa was getting interested in Mr. John Iverson, even if he *was* an old character of almost thirty!

"Who cares?" he muttered defiantly, pouring out so much paint remover that the fumes choked him when he forgot to turn his head aside.

"*You* do!" Annette snapped impatiently. "And so do I. I don't like that Iverson. I don't know why he's so anxious to get his hooks into this place, but I bet it isn't because his great-grand-daddy lived here! He's about as sentimental as a polar bear!"

"But she likes him!" Jinks peered at Lisa for-lornly through his paint-spattered lenses. "He's smart and a slick talker. He knows all the answers."

"I bet you know a few he doesn't! Look, Jinks"—Annette had an idea all of a sudden—"how about doing some showing off yourself?"

"You're kidding."

"No! Remember that little piece of ribbon onyx you gave her out of your rock collection for Christmas? She was tickled with it. Maybe you could find some other kind of gem up there near the mine, for her birthday."

"Hey! That's an idea!" Jinks exclaimed.

"I don't think the others would mind if you gave her a present. 'Specially when you didn't buy it."

"Yeah. There ought to be opals, agate, onyx, or even geodes, and I don't imagine the place has been combed over by many rock hounds!" Jinks was dreaming out loud.

"Anyhow, not by Mr. Iverson! I don't think he'd know an agate if it bit him!" Annette laughed.

"You're an angel," Jinks told her solemnly. "I'll get out there by sunup with my little hammer and pickax."

"And don't worry about Aunt Tish. I'll take her and Theresa in my car," Annette assured him.

For the rest of the day and evening, they exchanged a lot of knowing looks, and though John Iverson lingered till he was invited to dinner at the Kerrys', it didn't seem to dampen Jinks's spirits. He had fun with the other kids, singing along with the latest records, dancing the newest steps, and, in general, acting as if he hadn't a care in the world.

Mr. and Mrs. Kerry, watching the young people have a good time, sighed a little and went back to their account books to figure out how they could get along without the thousand dollars that the bank had refused to lend them.

CHAPTER 8

A Birthday Gift

Before daylight the next morning, Annette awoke to the sound of Jinks's sports car starting up across the way. She knew his motor. She had heard it often in the driveway next door at home.

She smiled to herself and turned over in bed for a few extra winks. Good luck, Jinks, she thought. Hope you find a super-duper hunk of something pretty to give her! Then she went back to sleep till Mrs. Kerry came upstairs to wake both girls an hour later.

Aunt Tish was already there, having a second breakfast and complaining between bites about Jinks's desertion. "Goodness knows where he ran off to so early in the morning! Why, the boy didn't even wait for the hotel dining room to open for breakfast! And he knows I'm depending on him to get me out there to paint!"

"We thought you'd be more comfortable in my car, with Theresa and the lamb having to go, too," Annette explained. "I'll go pick them up now, and come back for you."

Theresa wasn't waiting outside the station as she had promised. In fact, Annette didn't see anyone around, but the front gate was unlocked, so she knew Mr. Kerry must be there somewhere.

She went in, glancing with approval at the newly painted walls in the main room and the clean, scrubbed stones of the fireplace. The spot on the floor where Jinks had spilled the paint and splashed John Iverson's shoes was hardly noticeable.

She saw Mr. Kerry up on the roof, trying to fit some broken pieces of tile over one of the holes. He was quite busy, so she didn't interrupt him. She went back across the deserted courtyard toward the caretaker's house.

Marie and Charley were there, but they didn't

know where Theresa had gone. "Never mind, I'll find her," Annette told them, and she began to look around.

As she came close to the burned-out barn, she heard a soft hiss. It was Theresa, eyes dancing with mischief, hiding behind a tall barrel beside the doorway and beckoning to Annette. She laid a finger across her lips as a warning not to speak.

I suppose the lamb is doing something cute, Annette thought. She went over quietly to humor Theresa.

"Look at him!" Theresa whispered close to Annette's ear. "What game is he playing?" She pointed through the door, into shadowy depths.

Annette stole a cautious look into the barn. For a brief moment she couldn't see anything in its dark depths. Then she made out the figure of a man moving across the floor. He was stooping as he went, examining the flooring. He had some kind of a short iron bar in his hand which he thrust between the rough planks from time to time. He seemed to be trying to pry them up. But each time, the plank held firm, and he moved on again.

Then, as the man came into a patch of light from a small window in the hayloft, Annette saw that he was John Iverson. She clapped her hand over her mouth to stop a surprised exclamation. What was Iverson trying to do? Find something under a loose plank?

Maybe he's heard that his great-grandpappy hid some "jools" under the floor, she thought with a grin. Maybe that's why he wanted to buy the place from the Kerrys! I hope he finds 'em. They'll all belong to the Kerrys if he does. Or will they? She stopped "maybe-ing" hastily. John Iverson was at the far side of the barn now, and he might be turning back at any moment! "Come on," she whispered to Theresa. "We mustn't let him see us watching."

"Is it a game? I do not understand," Theresa whispered. But Annette drew her away to a safe distance, gave her a hug, and laughed. "Let's go get Esteban. Aunt Tish is waiting for us."

Before they left with the lamb, Marie brought a woven basket of homegrown corn and piñon nuts to Theresa to give to Lisa as their gift.

And she followed it up with a long string of instructions, finger-shaking, and solemn warnings to her small daughter in the Navajo language.

Theresa kept shaking her head, meekly, while her mother was speaking, and at the end she assured her solemnly, *"Do-dah!"* which seemed to satisfy her mother.

"What is this *do-dah*?" Annette asked her as they got into the car outside the station.

"It means 'no' in the Navajo language. It means, 'No, I will not go into the mine, which is the home of ghosts.'"

"Don't worry, hon," Annette said with a laugh. "Aunt Tish does her sketching on level ground. She'd never ask you to climb that hill to pose."

"That's good." Theresa was thoughtful. "Even for one dollar I would not go." She shuddered. "I do not wish to see the face of the one with the gold tooth. He's a bad spirit."

As Aunt Tish was stowing away her painting gear in the luggage compartment of the Monster, Annette told Lisa quietly about John Iverson's strange actions in the barn. For a moment, Lisa looked puzzled. Then she laughed. "Dad's been talking about rebuilding the barn one of these days, when things are going well. Mr. Iverson was probably testing the flooring to see if any of it would have to be replaced."

"I hadn't thought of that," Annette admitted.

Lisa giggled. "I suppose you thought he was doing something he shouldn't," she said. "Stop picking on the poor man just because he's more grown-up than some of the others."

Annette laughed. "I'm not picking on him, really. I only thought it looked funny. I'm sorry if I don't think he's the last word. I just can't, that's all!"

But they soon forgot John Iverson as the car rolled smoothly out beyond the town, up to the base of the flower-draped hillside crowned by the old mine buildings.

Lisa's friends had already arrived, and Karen and Janey were spreading the picnic lunch on a collapsible table under a feather-leafed acacia tree. The boys were scouting for juniper branches to use for the fire.

They were all noisily glad to see the latecomers, and there was a lot of picture-taking, comic poses by Billy Joe and Dave, and much confusion. But through it all, they all carefully refrained from mentioning a word about birthdays. They were saving the surprise for Mrs. Kerry's arrival with the home-baked cake she had promised.

Annette kept looking for some sign of Jinks, but he wasn't anywhere to be seen. Once, she thought she saw someone duck out of sight among the buildings up the hill, but the glimpse she had was so brief that she couldn't be sure who it was. Chances were that it was Jinks, she thought. The poor boy was probably having bad luck finding a pretty enough specimen of gemstone to offer Lisa.

Hope he doesn't stay away looking for it and miss all the fun, she thought, studying the old buildings. I'd go up and drag him down here if I could be sure it was Jinks I saw up there.

"Anyhow, I'm glad nobody told John Iverson there was to be a picnic. He won't be turning on the charm for Lisa while Jinks is out digging."

Annette made up her mind to look for Jinks. There was a chance he might be just around the corner of the road among the low hills. There were narrow tire tracks nearby that could belong to his car.

But just as she started off, she heard Lisa calling, and when she turned, her friend ran up to her.

"Did Jinks say anything last night about having an errand or something? I thought he said he would be coming to the picnic." She was pouting.

"He did, but I think he wanted to take care of something important first." Annette smiled mysteriously. "Don't worry, he'll show up soon!"

"Oh!" Lisa caught a hint that Annette knew something pleasant. She suspected it might be in connection with her birthday. "I didn't *think* he'd desert us—" She glanced past Annette suddenly and broke off. Annette turned to see what had attracted her attention.

It was John Iverson's convertible, and he was at the wheel. It was turning in off the highway.

"Mr. Iverson! I wanted to invite him, but I

didn't think he'd care about such juvenile things as picnics!"

Iverson had pulled up in his his car and was waving his cap to Lisa. He got out, while everyone stopped whatever he or she was doing and watched. Iverson lifted a cake from the rear floor of his car. It was unmistakably a birthday cake, lavishly decorated. He held it up and, with a flourish, started over toward the table as Karen and Janey clapped their hands with excitement.

"Oh!" Lisa looked thrilled. "He found out it was my birthday! Nobody else knew about it!"

And before Annette could tell her they *all* knew and had planned the picnic as a birthday surprise, Lisa was hurrying over to Iverson.

"Oh, fine!" Annette was angry with Iverson and with Lisa, too. But, most of all, she was angry with herself because Jinks wasn't there.

She stalked away and around the turn in the road without a backward look at the group oohing and aahing over the cake.

And there, sitting on a pile of granite rocks, his small hammer in hand, sat Jinks Bradley,

staring happily at something he was holding.

He saw Annette at almost the same time she saw him, and he beamed at her joyfully. "Look at this!" He held out the object on his palm. "Silicate of alumina!"

Annette ran to him. "Silly what?" she asked doubtfully.

"Silicate of—oh, shucks! Topaz! Look at the depth of that color. It's like her hair! Do you think she'll like it?" Jinks asked.

Annette took the crystal in her hand and looked closely at it. "It's lovely! Of course she will! Let's go right back and give it to her now!"

But a few minutes later, as they came up, a little breathless from hurrying, they stopped abruptly some yards away. John Iverson was handing a tissue-wrapped small package to Lisa while the others stood, watching unhappily. It was evident from the boys' scowls and the girls' pouts that John Iverson's gift-giving didn't sit well with Lisa's other friends.

Annette saw that Lisa was paying no attention to anyone but Iverson. She blushed as she took the gift and hesitated over removing the wrapping.

"Here, allow me!" John Iverson smiled into her eyes and ripped off the tissue to display a jeweler's box. Inside it, on soft cotton, lay what looked to Lisa like a plain egg-shaped stone.

"Why—uh—thanks!" Lisa murmured, wondering if this was a joke. Then as she turned it over, the two halves fell apart and lay glistening in the sunlight, reflecting rays of purple, lavender, and pale violet. "How lovely! What is it?"

Jinks, watching from a distance, knew what it was, but the others didn't. He had hunted for geodes many times, but the one Iverson had given Lisa was more spectacular than any of the ones he had found.

"Just one of nature's birthday gifts to a pretty lady. It's been lying around for several hundred years in the desert. I found it and had it split for you."

The others crowded around, exclaiming about the color and beauty of the crystals. Even Annette had to admit it was lovely.

When she looked for Jinks a few moments

later, he was gone. And his own offering, discarded, lay in the sand. She picked it up and put it into her pocket. No one else had noticed.

John Iverson was telling Lisa, "Your mother had some friends drop in, so I promised to bring the cake safely to you."

"You did a good job!" Lisa laughed.

Theresa had to see the pretty cake, so Aunt Tish let her stop posing and come for a look. "Mmm!" the little girl exclaimed. Never had there been such a cake! And she was to have some of it! She let go of Esteban's rope as she stared hungrily at its glory.

"Theresa! Quick!" It was Aunt Tish's bellow. "That dratted lamb! Up the hill! Catch him!"

Everyone looked quickly and laughed as Theresa started running wildly up the hill after her runaway, her long skirts almost tripping her and her arms waving wildly.

Only John Iverson scowled. And Annette, noticing it, wondered.

Theresa stopped suddenly, staring upward at the buildings of the old mine. Then she came stumbling wildly down, falling, getting up, and running again. But the lamb kept on upward among the flowers.

Theresa reached the road and threw herself into Annette's arms. "The ghost! I saw him! He will kill Esteban!"

"Here, here! Stop crying!" Iverson towered over Annette and the child. "Nothing's going to happen to your lamb. I'll go after him."

"I don't mind going, sir," Billy Joe suggested.

"I need the exercise." Iverson laughed, and before anyone else could speak, he was striding up the hill.

"He certainly is obliging, isn't he?" Lisa said to Janey, sighing.

"And good-looking!" Janey teased. "Lucky gal!"

But I still can't like him, Annette thought. She felt a little ashamed because she seemed so prejudiced.

She would have felt justified if she could have followed him up the hill and watched his meeting with the ghost.

CHAPTER 9

Another Gift

Annette watched with her arm around Theresa's shoulders as John Iverson strode up the hill to capture the runaway lamb.

"Don't worry, honey. He'll catch Esteban for you," she assured the little girl.

"He is a brave man who is not afraid of that wicked ghost," Theresa whispered, shivering.

Aunt Tish called impatiently, "Come on back here and let me finish this poster. I'll sketch Esteban in roughly for now."

So Annette led Theresa back to pose again for Aunt Tish.

There were a few giggles from Karen and

Janey as the lamb led John Iverson on a chase far
up the hillside. But when he went out of sight
behind the old mine shacks, they lost interest.
There were three hungry young men who wanted
to start eating the picnic lunch and the luscious
cake that topped it.

It was only Annette who wondered why it was
taking John Iverson so long to catch the lamb
and bring it back down the hill. "Maybe the
ghost wants to keep it for a pet," she told Lisa
with a grin.

"Personally, I don't think there's anyone at all
up there," Lisa confided. "I think Theresa saw
the wind blow the bushes, and her imagination
got busy."

But Lisa was wrong. John Iverson, holding
the lamb under his arm, was deep in a conference
with Gold-Tooth Shay.

"There was no sign of a trapdoor in the barn
floor," Iverson said, frowning. "I tried all the
boards, but there wasn't a loose one. I'll have to
get into the Indians' house somehow. It's near
the back wall, and the tunnel might lead out from

there and under the wall to where the river used to run."

"How you going to get in, with old Charley there ready with his rifle?" Shay asked. "You've got no excuse."

"I'll find one. And I'll do it soon," Iverson said firmly. "We can't take a chance on waiting too long. With all those kids down there, running in and out of the station helping Kerry, somebody may stumble on that tunnel entrance any time."

"Hey! One of them was poking around here," Shay said, "lookin' for something since early in the morning. Young, skinny kid in a fancy straw hat with a red band on it. Tourist, I guess."

"I know the one you mean. Bradley. Friend of that bright little dame who had the idea of opening an antiques shop. I'd like to wring her pretty neck!" Iverson's scowl showed that he meant it. "Hope you didn't let that Bradley boy spot you."

"He came near it a couple of times, but I ducked. He finally left with old Pete."

"Who's that?" Iverson frowned.

"Pete Wallace. They call him Pete the

Prospector around town. He's an old-timer. Comes in every now and then, with his moth-eaten burros, to raise a grubstake, he tells me. Always has some new claim, way over the hills someplace. Nobody ever makes a nickel on him, I'll bet."

"What's he doing with the kid, do you figure?" Iverson asked.

Shay chuckled. "Probably sellin' him a treasure map. He's got a lot of 'em. Gets five or ten dollars each from the suckers."

The lamb had begun to bleat loudly and struggle to get free of Iverson's grasp.

"I can't stop to talk anymore now. Somebody will be up to see what's keeping me and the lamb." He started away. "I'll see you later."

"Can't you leave that critter? I could use some fresh meat!" Shay eyed the lamb hungrily.

John Iverson didn't bother to answer. He flung a scowl at his partner before he started around the old shack and down the hill.

"Esteban!" Theresa ran to meet Iverson and the lamb with her arms outstretched. "You are safe! The ghost did not harm you!" And as

Iverson handed over the small, wriggling crea-
ture to its mistress, she clasped it in her arms and
hugged it till it baaed noisily.

Later, as Iverson and Lisa sat a little apart
from the others, finishing their slices of birthday
cake together, she told him, "You saved Aunt
Tish's life, too, sort of. If she hadn't been able to
finish that poster today and send it off to
Williams tomorrow to be printed for our antiques
shop, she'd have had a conniption."

"Really?" He looked as if he weren't quite as
pleased as Lisa about that.

Lisa noticed and her own spirits sank. "Do
you still think Dad is foolish to try to open the
shop? Nobody else seems to think he is."

This was Iverson's chance. "My dear Lisa, I
think he's taking a tremendous gamble! Suppose
there's another fire, after the antiques are there."

"I hadn't thought of that!" Lisa was worried.

"Of course, he could take out insurance. But
do you realize what the cost would be?" He stole
a look at her worried face. "The premium on
valuable antiques is enormous!" And he added

slyly, "Of course, it's none of my business, I suppose, but I'm very fond of"—he paused meaningfully—"his family. And I hate to see him lose more than he already has lost."

A couple of hours later, driving home beside Annette in the Monster, Lisa told her friend what John Iverson had said.

"Do you think I should tell Dad?" she asked worriedly.

Annette was silent for a moment. Then she said, very matter-of-factly, "I think your father is a sensible person. I think he'd take Mr. John Iverson's advice with a grain of salt, especially since Mr. John Iverson is so very anxious to move into the station himself."

Lisa frowned. "But if there's another fire—"

Annette cut her short. "If there is, I hope Mr. Iverson is a long way off, or somebody might ask him where he happened to be when it started!"

"There you go!" Lisa's chin set hard. "Everything he says is wrong to you, because you don't like him. But when Jinks Bradley deliberately stays away from my birthday surprise party, you make excuses for him. And *I* think he's just plain rude and—and childish!"

"He stayed away to find something out in that hot desert that would be good enough to give you for a birthday present—that's how childish he is!" Annette snapped.

"Oh," Lisa said weakly. "I—I'm sorry. I didn't know."

"And when he came back with this"—Annette took out the small chunk of topaz and dropped it into Lisa's hand—"he saw Mr. Grandstand Iverson making a big deal out of presenting you with something a lot more showy. So he threw this one away and went on looking."

"But it's lovely, really. I wish he hadn't felt that way about it. If you see him before I do, would you tell him that I think it's just as nice as the geode?"

"Nope!" Annette threw her a roguish glance. "You've got to tell him yourself, if you can both stop being so bashful!" And she refused to be coaxed.

But when they were swinging in the glider a little before suppertime, waiting for Aunt Tish

and Jinks to come over, Lisa was still jittery about what she was going to say about her birthday gift.

Annette stopped swinging. "Here he comes now. Trot down to the gate, where only the grasshoppers and tree toads can hear, and make your little speech." And she pushed Lisa toward the steps.

Jinks was wearing a coat and tie and carrying his hat in one hand and a strangely shaped, chunky package in the other. It was loosely wrapped in newspaper.

He stopped outside the gate as Lisa came slowly down the path to him.

Annette swung silently, trying not to listen as they met, but Pine Mesa was in its usual late afternoon silence and she couldn't help hearing.

"I suppose you've had all the birthday gifts you want by this time," Jinks was saying.

Annette winced. This wasn't a very promising start!

Lisa laughed a little. "I've had some very lovely ones, thank you. And especially one—"

Annette relaxed. Good girl! she thought. Neat!

But Jinks was saying in an unexpectedly loud voice, "Yeah! I saw the big four-flusher giving it to you!"

"Jinks!" Now Lisa was raising her voice, too.

Goodness! Annette thought weakly. Here we go!

"That's what he is!" Jinks seemed to be angry. "I saw that geode myself yesterday in Babbitt's Curio Store. Iverson didn't find it. He *bought* it. And lied about it!"

"What if he did? At least he *gave* it to me. He didn't change his mind and throw it away without seeing if I liked it! He didn't run off and sulk!"

"Ow!" Annette pulled a pillow over her head to shut out the angry words. "I won't listen. I'll count to a hundred. Maybe by then they'll be ready to make up! One—two—"

But by the time she reached fifty, the porch boards vibrated under the heels of an angry young woman, and Lisa plunked herself down in the glider beside her.

Annette moved the pillow and looked out at Lisa questioningly. The streetlight across the way had just come on, and something like a tear seemed to be rolling down each of Lisa's cheeks and reflecting its light.

Annette asked warily, "Well?"

"He's simply impossible!" Lisa's voice was sharp.

Annette sat up. "Did he go away again?"

Lisa nodded vigorously. "And I hope he stays away!" She sat frowning, while, unheeded, the tears splashed onto the package in her lap.

"What's in that?" Annette touched it.

"Some kind of a birthday present, I suppose. He just pushed it at me and stalked off. I would have thrown it after him if it hadn't been so heavy that it might have hurt!"

"Let's see what it is. I bet it's pretty!" Annette was trying to take Lisa's mind off her hurt feelings.

Lisa sniffed a couple of times and then pulled the string off the newspaper-wrapped object. When it lay uncovered in her lap, she sat and stared at it with complete bewilderment.

"Why, it's only a chunk of rock!" Annette exclaimed.

Lisa's eyes flashed. "I suppose he thinks he's being funny!" She jumped to her feet and rushed to the top of the steps. The rock went flying through the air, landed on the walk, and rolled a couple of feet toward the gate before it came to a stop. "That's what I think of him and his silly jokes!"

She turned and rushed into the house and up to her room.

"Now what?" Annette sighed to herself. She was tempted to go across to the hotel and scold Jinks for the way he had acted. But just about the time she had made up her mind to start, she heard his car start somewhere back in the hotel garage.

A moment later, he had roared out in his car and was driving away fast.

In the morning when Aunt Tish came over after breakfast, she told the Kerrys, "I don't know what's got into that boy of mine! He insisted on taking those posters into Williams last night, instead of waiting till this morning."

"I guess the sooner the printing shop gets them, the sooner they'll be copied and we can post them around." Mrs. Kerry smiled. "No doubt he thought of that."

But Lisa just wrinkled her nose disdainfully and went on drying the dishes.

Mr. Kerry came striding in. He had two chunks of rock in his hands and a strange expression on his face. "Where did this silver ore come from?" he demanded of anyone who might know.

"Silver ore?" Annette had seen at once that it was the despised chunk of rock, now split into two pieces from hitting the paved walk. "Is that what it is?"

"Look!" Mr. Kerry laid the ore on the table and traced a wide gray streak that ran through the rock from one end to the other in a strangely twisted pattern. He scratched the streak with his finger, and it shone silvery in the morning sunlight. "It's rich silver ore. And I nearly fell over it just now in our yard!"

Annette glanced at Lisa, who looked stunned.

Mrs. Kerry and Aunt Tish stared at it, and

Aunt Tish sniffed audibly. "It doesn't look like much to me."

"I suppose not," Mr. Kerry said with a smile, "but if you ever come across a piece of rock that looks like this, run to an assayer's office. You may be on the way to being rich!"

"I thought it was just rock." Lisa had found her tongue at last. Annette had almost thought she never would. "Jinks gave it to me last night—for a birthday joke, I thought."

"Jinks?" Mr. Kerry almost shouted. "Where did he find it? Where is he?"

"Gone to Williams," Mrs. Kerry told him.

"Did he tell you where he found it?" Mr. Kerry asked Lisa.

"I—I'm afraid I didn't ask him. We had a little spat, and he left before I even looked at it."

"I thought something like that had happened, the way he rushed off with those posters," boomed Aunt Tish, shaking her head. "These children!"

Lisa looked as if she were about to say something angry to Aunt Tish, so Annette spoke up quickly. "I'm pretty sure he found it up near where we had the picnic. He was looking around on those hills nearly all day yesterday."

"Near the old mine?" Mr. Kerry looked excited.

Annette nodded. "All around there. He was looking for a present for Lisa."

Mr. Kerry weighed the ore in his hand thoughtfully. Then he dropped the chunk with the silver vein into his pocket. "Don't mention this to anyone, any of you. I'm going to put in a call to Jinks at Williams and find out just where this came from. After that—we'll see!" His eyes were shining with excitement. "Maybe Pine Mesa is going to be back on the map again, after all!"

He hurried out and across the street to the hotel, leaving four excited voices eagerly discussing the situation.

But Jinks Bradley had not checked in at the hotel where he had planned to stay. And Mr. Kerry's calls to the other three hotels in Williams, where he might have registered instead, brought the same answer.

There was no one named Bradley staying at any of them.

CHAPTER 10

Trickery

"I'm so excited!" Lisa's face glowed. They were waiting for her father to come back across the street from talking to Jinks Bradley in Williams. Then she looked serious. "Do you think Jinks will ever forgive me for being so rude to him last night? I'm ashamed of myself."

"Don't ask me about him!" Annette held up her hands in surrender. "I've quit guessing about either of you!"

They hung onto the front gate and watched the hotel entrance till they saw Mr. Kerry come out.

"Oh, golly!" Lisa cried. "He doesn't look very happy about it. I wonder what's the matter."

Lon Kerry stopped to speak to Sheriff Martinez, then slowly crossed the street.

Lisa couldn't wait for him to get close. "What did Jinks say about the ore, Dad?" she called.

"Couldn't locate him. I tried several hotels but he hadn't registered at any of them. I can't understand where he could have stopped."

"Maybe he found a cheaper place to stay." Annette smiled knowingly. "I doubt if Aunt Tish gave him much money to spend."

"Well, wherever he is," Lon Kerry said, shaking his head, "it looks as if we'll just have to wait till he gets back to ask him any questions about this." He took the chunk of ore out of his pocket and gave it to Lisa. "Better put this away for a couple of days. Miss Bradley thinks he'll wait over at Williams for the posters and won't be back before Thursday."

Lisa took the rock almost reverently and stood holding it on her outstretched palms looking at it. "I never saw silver ore before. It's been a long time since anybody found any around here."

"That looks like a very good specimen!"

John Iverson had come up, unnoticed. "Where did you find that?" He spoke lightly, almost indifferently.

"In our own front yard here!" Lisa laughed.

"Well, aren't you the lucky ones!" Iverson's mouth widened with a thin smile, but Annette saw his eyes narrow into those snaky slits again, and her spine felt a shiver as it had before. "A silver mine right in your own yard!"

"I'm afraid it's not as simple as that!" Lon Kerry laughed, but there was a hollow ring to his laugh. "That was a birthday gift, but we haven't found out yet where Jinks got hold of it."

"Probably in a curio store," Iverson said promptly. "Babbitt's has quite a collection of ore."

Annette thought wickedly, You could tell us all about what Babbitt's sells, Mr. Four-flusher. Like geodes, for instance! But she continued to look innocently at Iverson.

"I hadn't thought about Babbitt's," Lon Kerry said, frowning. He was disappointed. He had begun to build a few dreams on that chunk of ore. "I imagine that's about where he got it."

"It doesn't matter where it came from," Lisa said coolly, with a little toss of her head. "I think it's lovely, and I'm going to display it at the shop when we open, right next to my pretty geode!" She flashed a little smile at Iverson as she mentioned the geode.

"Let's get into our work clothes." Annette drew Lisa away from the gate. "All the kids are going to be at the station this morning like eager little beavers."

"I'm glad you have plenty of help. I'd like to stick around myself today and lend a hand, but I have some bank business that may keep me all morning," John Iverson told Mr. Kerry as the girls disappeared into the house.

"Don't give it a thought, John." Lon Kerry smiled. "You helped a lot yesterday morning. I appreciate it more than you know."

But when Lon Kerry had gone down the street toward the station a few minutes later, it wasn't the bank that Iverson visited. He went instead directly to the livery stable where he had hired a horse the other night. And when he rode out through the alley behind the stable, he stayed off the main street till he was clear of town. Then he struck out for the old mine at a lively canter.

Gold-Tooth Shay was asleep in the highest shack, wrapped in his blankets and snoring loudly. Iverson could hear him long before he got to the building.

Iverson stirred him with the toe of his boot. "Wake up! You going to sleep all day?"

Shay rolled out of his blankets and got lazily to his feet, blinking and yawning. "Had a late night," he explained. "Got into a card game with old Pete over at his camp. Turned in around daylight." He glanced out the door and saw that it was still early in the day. "How come you're out here this time of the morning?"

"I want to know where that Bradley kid spent his time around here yesterday. Looks like he found himself some rich ore out this way."

"You don't say!" Shay was wide-awake instantly. "Well, he was all over the west side of the hill. Seemed to be keepin' out of sight of the rest of the kids. And come to think of it, I saw him chippin' the rocks with a little hammer, like he was prospectin'!"

"Whereabouts was that?" Iverson snapped.

"Oh, here an' there." He eyed Iverson sharply. "You figurin' on stakin' a claim if you locate where he found the rich stuff?"

"Sure! If *he* didn't stake it himself and register his claim! We've got to look around and find out."

"What do we want to do a lot of mining for?" Shay asked. "We got more cash somewhere in that station than you would dig out of the ground around here. You giving up on that?"

"Not at all!" Iverson glared at Shay. "But that ore I saw this morning is rich, I tell you."

"Okay. We'll look around soon as I get some grub in me." Shay yawned and rubbed his eyes with his fists.

Iverson stared. A silver watchband encircled Shay's thick wrist tightly. "Where did you get that?"

Shay looked startled, then grinned as he turned his wrist to display a smart wristwatch. "Won it off old Pete, playin' pinochle last night."

"Let's have a look." Iverson held out his hand. Shay flipped his prize to his partner.

He could see at once that it was a very good watch. "Good make. Worth quite a bit." He turned it over quickly to look at the back. "'J. B. Bradley,'" he read out. "Why, Pete must have gotten this from the Bradley kid yesterday! No wonder it was too tight for your wrist if it belonged to that skinny kid!"

Shay rubbed his wrist where the band had cut in. "Seems likely that's where he got it. He didn't say. Only that he took it in place of cash for somethin' he sold."

"Sounds like it might have been a map he sold. A map of the place where Bradley found that silver ore!" Iverson exclaimed.

"Yeah! Maybe . . . only, the kid didn't come back here to do any diggin' after the time he left with Pete. And the old feller told me all his maps are phonies," Shay said.

"Maybe *he* thinks so! But it looks like this time he had one that was the real thing, without knowing it. And I think we'll find out that

Bradley has the claim all staked out and filed in town right now!" Iverson cried.

But when they searched the hillside for a long distance in each direction where it might have been, they found no trace of a claim having been staked. There were only chipped rocks here and there, and traces of Jinks's footprints.

"Let's go talk to the old man. We'll see what he has to tell us." Iverson looked grim.

A short time later, they tramped up to the location of the old prospector's camp. But the camp was deserted. Old Pete and his burros were gone. Some empty tin cans and the blackened stones he had used to encircle his cooking fire were all that was left.

"Shall we follow him?" Shay asked. "I'm pretty good at trailing."

But Iverson shook his head impatiently. "Let him go."

He had just found something, a little apart from the camp, lying on the side of the trail that showed sharp marks of both the burros' hooves and the miner's boots. It was an old burlap sack.

Its rotted bottom had given way, and there were chunks of ore scattered about as if they had dropped through the hole.

Iverson picked up a chunk of the ore and studied it.

There was a narrow twisted streak of gray across its face. He scratched it with his knife to be sure, and the scratch showed bright silver under the dullness. It was silver ore, sure enough, and similar to the kind he had seen in Lisa's hands that morning! He dropped it and picked up another chunk.

This time there was no vein of silver. This was a chunk of granite, and there were tiny flecks of gold, even one tiny nugget, embedded in it.

Still another piece that he picked up bore square-shaped crystals of galena on its surface and was heavy with lead. He threw it aside.

Shay came over. "More stuff from the location where the kid found his?" he asked eagerly.

Iverson shook his head. "From a lot of loca-tions. Old Pete's a collector. And unless I've missed my guess, it wasn't a map he sold young

Bradley, but one of these samples. No wonder we couldn't find where he dug it. It may have come from a hundred miles away!"

"Then, we did all our hikin' around for nothin'?" Shay was disgusted.

"Maybe not." Iverson's shrewd brain was beginning to work. "Maybe not at all!" He was smiling again.

It was the middle of the afternoon when John Iverson drove up outside the station.

Annette was out front, sweeping the faded fallen clusters of pink tamarisk blossoms from the sidewalk. Iverson strode past her with only a slight nod. He evidently had something important on his mind.

Inside she could hear gusts of laughter and the sound of Billy Joe playing his banjo to entertain the others while they worked. They were just about finished with the cleaning, and Mrs. Kerry had brought a gallon of homemade ice cream and some of Marie's cookies as a reward.

Annette finished the sweeping in a whirl and hurried toward the door. She didn't want to miss the treat.

But just as she reached the door, she met Lisa and her father hurrying out, followed by John Iverson.

Lisa looked radiant. "Annette! Mr. Iverson met a man who saw Jinks digging on the west side of the mine hill yesterday! That may be where he found the ore!"

"We're going there now to see if he staked out any spot," her father added. "Mr. Iverson is lending us his car."

"Isn't he going to help you look?" Annette looked surprised. "I should think the three of you could cover more ground."

"I'm expecting a long-distance call from my bank on the Coast," he said with a smile. "Why don't *you* go?"

"Oh, do!" Lisa begged Annette. "There's plenty of room in this lovely big car."

"I think I *will* go, at that!" Annette agreed. She thrust her broom into Iverson's hands. "You can have my share of the ice cream and cookies."

Iverson stood scowling after her, with the broom in his hand, as she climbed into his car with the Kerrys. Then as they drove off, he tossed the broom aside and, instead of going into the station, walked slowly up the street to his hotel. He would wait there to hear from Shay how their plan worked.

Aunt Tish was rocking back and forth nervously in one of the hotel's ancient cane rockers as Iverson came up onto the porch.

"What's the news from the boy?" he asked genially.

Aunt Tish shook her head. "Not a word! I don't understand it. He promised me he'd call the moment he reached Williams. But not a word! And no trace of him anywhere."

"Maybe he couldn't get the work done in Williams," Iverson suggested easily, "and drove on to Flagstaff or even to Phoenix."

Aunt Tish stopped rocking to stare at him. "Why, that must be it! Why didn't I think of that?" She reached over and patted Iverson's arm. "You're a very clever young man, Mr. Iverson."

But Aunt Tish had no idea just how clever he really was!

CHAPTER 11

Silver Strike

From the old mine shack high on the hillside, Gold-Tooth Shay watched Lon Kerry and the two girls arrive in John Iverson's convertible and park at the foot of the hill.

They stopped to talk a few minutes, scanning the rocky slope. Then they split up. Kerry went one way on the hill, while each of the girls took a different path among the wildflowers. They all scanned the ground as they moved slowly upward.

Shay chuckled as he saw Lon Kerry approach a cluster of boulders about halfway up to the entrance of the old mine shaft. "Come on, Kerry!" he urged softly. "Just a few feet more this way, pal, and you've found it!"

A moment later, he wore a wide grin as Lon Kerry stopped to stare at something near a tall rock.

He picked up what looked from above like a small chunk of rock. Shay chuckled again. He knew what it was. He had helped put it there! It was silver ore, rich with the metal.

"Lisa! Annette! Come here! I've found it!" Kerry's voice came clearly to Shay.

"Sucker!" Shay grinned as he watched the girls hurry through the wild lupines to Lon Kerry and heard their squeals of excitement and delight.

The girls hugged each other, laughing, and even picked up a couple of chunks of the ore themselves to show Mr. Kerry.

Then, to Shay's delight, Lon Kerry wrote out what Shay guessed rightly was a discovery notice and weighted it down securely with a rock on the flat top of one of the boulders. It was just what John Iverson had hoped Kerry would do.

When that was done, he and the two girls stepped off the boundaries of the claim, with the cluster of rocks in the center. They made small cairns of stones to mark the sides and ends of the claim. Then they struck branches, from the clump of mesquite nearby, into the top of each of the cairns to act as boundary posts.

Next, to Shay's surprise, they marked off a second claim, touching the first and centered by a lone juniper.

He waited patiently till they had driven away again in Iverson's car before he went cautiously down the hill. He was curious to see whose name was on the discovery notices they had posted.

The first claim was in J. B. Bradley's name, and the second in Kerry's.

Shay grinned. "Well, that ties them both in. John'll be tickled about that!" He hurried up to the shack to wait for Iverson to come.

In town at that moment, Iverson was watching from his hotel window as his car pulled up at the Kerry gate, and three happy, excited people piled out. Mrs. Kerry ran to meet them, and Mr. Kerry showed her a chunk of ore from his pocket. Then he went on up the street, while the two girls and Mrs. Kerry went into the house, chattering cheerfully. There was no question in Iverson's

mind about where Lon Kerry was going now. He was headed straight for the domed county court-house where records were filed. He was going to register a mining claim!

John Iverson slipped into his coat, adjusted his expensive Panama hat at an angle, and strolled down the stairs to the lobby.

The day clerk was yawning behind his desk. Iverson put down his room key and leaned on the desk.

"Wonder what's going on at the Kerrys'," he said idly. "He borrowed my car to take the girls for a ride, and just now he came back all excited and showed his wife a chunk of ore or some-thing. Could be he's struck something rich, from the fuss they were making. I saw them from my window."

"Hey!" The clerk's eyes went wide. "Silver?"

"I don't know. But I think I'll look him up and find out. I'd like to get in on something like that!"

And John Iverson went out and up the street after Lon Kerry.

The clerk stared after him a minute and then

turned to the desk phone. "Hello, Delia! Get me the *Pine Mesa Clarion*."

And in no time at all the news had started to circulate that it looked mightily like Lon Kerry had struck somethin' rich out west of town.

Lon Kerry was still filling out a government form when Sheriff Martinez came into the recorder's office. "What's all this about you striking it rich?" he demanded jovially.

"How did you hear that? Why—I'm just filing the claims now!" Lon Kerry was amazed.

"I dunno how it got around," Sheriff Martinez said, grinning widely, "but I heard it from four different people!"

Lon Kerry took the ore sample from his pocket. "I haven't had it assayed yet, but I hardly need to."

Sheriff Martinez's eyes bugged out. "I'll say you don't! This looks like some of the 'float' we used to pick up out Colorado way twenty years ago!"

"Looks like my luck has changed," Mr. Kerry admitted.

"Mr. Kerry!" It was the editor of the *Pine Mesa Clarion*. "How about a story on your discovery?

Any objections if we give it to the wire services?"

"Why—no. Go ahead. But I don't want to claim it was my discovery. It was a young man who's visiting us, who ran across the pay ore."

"Sure, Mr. Kerry! What's his name? Where can I talk to him?" The editor was persistent.

"Bradley—J. B. Bradley. They call him Jinks. I'm not sure just where he is now, but I believe he's due back in town in a day or so. You can talk to him then."

"Thanks!" The newspaper man hurried off. He almost ran over John Iverson in his haste to return to the newspaper office and get the story onto the presses for the morning edition.

John Iverson knew him. He was glad to see the editor of the local newspaper in such a frenzy of excitement. The more publicity Lon Kerry and young Bradley received, the better.

He was conveniently near the marble steps of the county courthouse as Lon Kerry came out.

"What's this I hear?" He saluted Mr. Kerry.

Mr. Kerry nodded, smiling from ear to ear. "We found it! The boy's discovery was out there, on the west of the mine hill. I've filed a claim for him—and one of my own!"

"Well, great!" John Iverson shook hands with a show of cordiality. "Glad I could be a little help."

"A little? If you hadn't given me the tip—but you know how grateful I am!" Lon Kerry was deeply in earnest. "And I intend to declare you in for a quarter interest. We're going to my lawyer right now to draw up the papers!"

"Whoa! I've got something to say about it!" Iverson held back. "I can't allow you to do a thing like that—just for a vague tip."

"I owe it to you," Kerry said stubbornly. "And I make a point of paying my debts."

"No!" Iverson shook his head firmly. "I admit that it's a temptation. I'm not a rich man, as I've told you. I have *some* money, of course." He paused, with a sly glance at Kerry's distressed face. "Tell you what we'll do. . . ."

"Whatever you say, but I insist on your having twenty-five percent of my claim!"

"All right, then," Iverson agreed. "I'll take it. But I want to *buy* in. I don't want it as a gift."

"But, Iverson, how can we fix a price? All we've seen so far is 'float.' Maybe it won't turn out to be worth sinking a shaft!" Kerry reasoned.

"I'll risk a thousand dollars. What do you say?" Lon Kerry frowned over it a moment; then, as he saw Iverson's determined expression, he sighed and gave in.

"You're a true friend, John," Kerry said humbly. "I've known men all my life here in Pine Mesa who are supposed to be my friends, and I doubt if more than one or two of them would be as generous as you are."

Kerry's attorney, Sam Franklin, agreed after a look at the ore sample that Iverson was getting a bargain. "Wish *I* had a chance to come in on it," he said with a chuckle as he drew up the legal papers.

Iverson signed the check with a flourish. It would be three or four days before it would clear and come bounding back, marked NO ACCOUNT. Before then, he hoped to finish up his business in Pine Mesa and be far away.

"I'd like to draw against this right now," Kerry told the bank cashier a few minutes later.

Outside, in full view of the cashier, Iverson was getting into his expensive car. "Of course, Lon, I'm sure it's okay," the cashier assured him genially. "If Iverson was willing to pay five thousand cash for that broken-down old station of yours, he's sure to have a measly thousand in the bank! You lucky dog!"

"Lucky is right," Lon Kerry agreed soberly.

It was a happy family that gathered at the Kerry supper table. Mr. and Mrs. Kerry were planning to go to the reservation the next day and rehire the Navajo workers to start repairing the roof. The expensive tiles that would add a picturesque touch had already been ordered and paid for. The work could start at once.

There was only one cloud in the sky. No one had heard from Jinks. Aunt Tish was angry with him and worried about her posters. The least he could have done, she had reminded them half a dozen times, was to have telephoned her at the hotel. But that was the younger generation. . . .

"When he does show up," Annette told Lisa as

they sat on the porch after supper, "I intend to
tell him what I think of him!"

"I may not even speak to him at all," Lisa said
with a sniff.

A shadowy figure came hurrying across the
street from the hotel. For a moment, Annette
thought that it might be Jinks, but as the man
came closer, she recognized the hotel night clerk.

He stopped at the gate. "Miss Annette?" he
called. "There's a phone call for you."

"Thanks! Be right with you." She laughed and
turned to Lisa. "That's probably Aunt Lila calling from Hollywood to see what mischief we've
gotten into so far!" Lisa smiled as Annette hurried down to the gate and started across the street
with the room clerk.

"Hollywood call?" she asked.

"Nope. Some hospital in Williams. Nurse says
it's important."

There was only one person whom she might
know in Williams. She ran the rest of the way to
the telephone.

CHAPTER 12

The Hero

Mr. Bradley had an accident on the road two nights ago, but he was all right now, the nurse told Annette over the phone. "Just a bump on his head and a bruised knee."

"Thank goodness, that's all!" She remembered how fast he had driven out of Pine Mesa.

"The doctor made him stay quiet in bed for a couple of days, till he could be sure he had no concussion. But he's ready to go home now, if you don't mind coming to get him."

Annette was puzzled. "Isn't he well enough to drive, nurse?"

"It isn't that, miss. His car has a broken axle

and is being repaired, but the garage here is shorthanded and it won't be ready till Saturday. He thought you might—"

"Okay, I'll start as soon as I can in the morning," Annette promised. "What shall I tell his aunt about the accident?"

"He says please don't tell *anyone* about it," the nurse told her. "He thinks he'd rather talk to you first."

"Oh, all right," Annette agreed. Now she was convinced he had been speeding. He probably wanted her to help make up a story for Aunt Tish. But she wouldn't. Walking back across the street to the Kerry house she told herself, rather grimly, that it was time Jinks grew up. She meant to tell him so on their way back from Williams.

It was long before daylight when Annette slid out of her bed and gathered her clothes together to tiptoe out of the room without awakening her friend. Fortunately, Lisa had assumed that the phone call had come from Aunt Lila.

Annette dressed hastily before the still-warm kitchen range with its banked fire. She didn't dare make herself any breakfast, for fear that the Kerrys might hear her and come down.

She downed a couple of yesterday's dough-nuts and hastily scribbled a note. "Dear folks," it began, "I have to take a little trip on important business. I'll be back long before dark. Love, Annette."

She propped the note against the sugar bowl and let herself noiselessly out the back door.

Annette guided her sleek, white sports car through the deserted main street. She drove out onto the highway to Williams as dawn was beginning to break.

She was feeling a hollow sensation by the time she drove into the desert town. She hadn't stopped anywhere to eat breakfast, and now it was almost lunchtime.

She had no trouble finding the hospital.

Jinks was sitting on a stone bench outside the gate, his traveling bag beside him, as she drew up. He had a lump over one eye and a black-and-blue spot on his chin.

"Hi!" He looked sheepish. "Much obliged for

coming, 'Nette." He tossed his bag in the back-seat and climbed in beside her.

"You're a sight!" Annette commented frankly.

"Yeah, I suppose so." He stole a look at himself in the rearview mirror and fingered his bumped head gingerly. "You didn't tell anybody I ran off the road, did you?"

"Of course not! Speeding?"

Jinks nodded. "Dopey trick. Dunno what got into me."

"What about Aunt Tish's posters?" she asked, turning the car back toward Pine Mesa.

"Oh—" Jinks groaned unhappily. "They got stepped on in the ditch when the highway patrol found me. Gosh, she'll be sore! Maybe you could get her to make a couple more—"

"Seems to me that's up to you to do." Annette spoke a bit sharply. She was getting tired of babying Jinks.

"Yeah, I guess so." Jinks sounded gloomy.

"Let's stop and eat," Annette said suddenly. "There's a clean-looking place up ahead." But when they got to it, there were crowds of cars

in its parking lot, and more lining the curb.

"Looks like a full house," Jinks observed. "We'd better try the next."

They went on and found the next small restaurant just as crowded.

But when they came to the third, half a mile on, Annette spotted a small parking space just large enough for the Monster and whipped into it. "This is it. I can't go another foot without food," she announced.

It was a noisy bunch of customers, and Annette noticed that almost all of them were men—some well dressed, some in work clothes, and even several bewhiskered ones who looked as if they had been away from civilization a long time.

The small radio behind the counter was making a large noise as they entered. The announcer sounded a bit hysterical. "They're coming in by the dozens, folks. Up from the dude ranches, out of the mountains. News spreads fast, and this is the biggest thing that's happened out our way since the days of Geronimo!"

The brisk waitress paused to listen as she was

clearing the counter in front of Annette and Jinks. "Imagine that! A real silver strike! And right out in our desert!"

"The old mining town of Pine Mesa is back on the map again!" shouted the radio announcer. "And *I'm* on my way! Whoopee!" The sound cut off suddenly.

"Pine Mesa! When did that happen?" Jinks looked at Annette, startled.

She stared at him in surprise. Then she started to laugh, and she laughed so hard that Jinks was alarmed. "Annette! What's the matter? You're hysterical!"

She stopped laughing suddenly. "Why, of course you wouldn't know! You've been shut up in a hospital!"

"Know what? About somebody finding silver?"

"Not *somebody*! *You!*" Annette pointed a finger at him. "You, Jinks Bradley!"

Jinks was bewildered. "But I don't see—"

"For those who haven't heard," another radio announcer spoke up, "here are the details of the big silver strike at Pine Mesa!" And while Jinks sat slack-jawed, listening unbelievingly, the romantic tale of his discovery of the rich ore unfolded.

Annette listened, smiling. But when she turned to speak to Jinks, she saw him elbowing his way frantically through the crowd toward the door. She took a last gulp of coffee and hurried after him.

She caught up with him outside the café. He looked sick and scared.

"Whatever is the matter? I should think you'd be delighted! Were you trying to keep it a secret or something?"

"Gosh, Annette!" Jinks's face was white. "There's been a horrible mistake. I didn't find that ore. I swapped my wristwatch for it with an old miner!"

"Oh, no!" Annette moaned. "Don't kid about it, Jinks Bradley! You *are* kidding, aren't you?" she asked anxiously. "You really found it on the west side of the mine hill, didn't you?"

"No. I told you where I got it."

"But Mr. Kerry picked up several pieces just

like it out there yesterday. Lisa and I were with him," Annette explained.

Jinks shook his head grimly. "I can't help that. It couldn't have come from there. Old Pete told me he had carted it around for years with other souvenirs."

"I think we ought to get back to Pine Mesa and talk to Mr. Kerry just as soon as we can," Annette said. "There's something awfully funny about the whole thing! Poor Mr. Kerry! He'll be so disappointed. And so will Mr. Iverson, though I don't care about *him*."

"What's he got to do with it?" Jinks scowled.

"He bought part of Mr. Kerry's claim. Paid a thousand dollars for it," Annette told him gloomily, as she drove on toward Pine Mesa.

"What claim?" Jinks demanded.

"The place where we found the silver ore," Annette explained impatiently, "near the mine. Where we thought yours came from."

"But it didn't come from around Pine Mesa, I tell you! Old Pete said it was from Colorado."

"Well, we found some just like it, where you

were chipping away at the rocks, day before yesterday."

Jinks gave a startled exclamation. "Hey! If you *did*, Mr. Kerry's really struck it rich! Old Pete said that was just about the richest ore he ever got hold of."

"Well, hooray for our side!" Annette cried. "Gosh, Jinks! You had me worried for a while. But now I feel lots better, knowing the Kerrys have really got themselves something!"

"That's swell! I hope they make a million!"

"Huh!" Annette laughed. "You won't be doing so badly yourself! He registered a claim for you, too, right in the same place."

"Gee!" Jinks swallowed hard, and his eyes were enormous behind the thick lenses. Then he beamed. "Hey! Can't you build a fire under this heap? I want to get back and talk to Lisa!"

Pine Mesa had changed a lot in the two days since Jinks had last seen it. Crowds of people streamed through the streets, spilling off the sidewalks into the honking traffic.

It was a good-natured, noisy crowd—men and

women of all descriptions and a horde of youngsters. They had parked their cars in every avail-
able space on the main street and up along the
side streets. Bumper to bumper were trucks,
pickups, house trailers with lace curtains, expensive convertibles, foreign cars, and Model A's.

A newsboy thrust a special edition of the
Clarion at Annette as she stopped for cross traffic. Then, while she fumbled in her purse, Jinks
flipped a coin to the boy and the boy got a good
look at him. "Hey! Here he is! Here's the guy
who made the strike!" he shouted to everyone.
"It's Jinks! Jinks Bradley! Here!"

Jinks's face was like a desert sunset. "Gosh,
Annette! Go on—drive!" he urged her. But it
was too late. Several other youngsters had
crowded around, some hanging on to the rear
bumper and some climbing on to the front. And
all were yelling, "Jinks! Jinks! Here's Jinks!"

All Annette could do was sit and laugh, as
Billy Joe and Dave and several of Lisa's other
teenage friends swooped down on the car and
dragged Jinks out.

In spite of his struggles, they put him up on their shoulders and started down the street, followed by a dozen small boys shouting, "Jinks! Jinks! Here's the boy who found it!" Traffic came to a complete standstill.

It wasn't till they had gone the length of Main Street and back to the hotel that they decided to let Jinks down. He had given up struggling a long time before and was actually enjoying his publicity by the time the boys tired of their clowning and dumped him off without ceremony.

He started to go into the hotel but hesitated. He still had some explaining to do to Aunt Tish. A glance across the street showed Annette sitting alone on the porch. He decided it wouldn't do any harm to postpone the reckoning with his aunt.

He went across the street and up to the porch.

"Nobody around." Annette swung in the glider. "They went to the reservation to order some more chairs like the ones that were burned and to hire some Navajos to work on the roofing."

"Lisa go, too?" Jinks was disappointed. He

had been hoping Lisa had seen his triumphal procession.

Annette nodded. Then she yawned sleepily and got to her feet. "If you don't mind, I think I'll take a nap. It's been a long day."

Jinks looked conscience-stricken. "Gosh, Annette, I didn't get around to telling you how much I appreciate your coming to get me and all."

Annette smiled sleepily. "Better get squared away with Aunt Tish before you lose your nerve."

"Yeah. Guess I might as well. Hope she won't be too sore! See you later." He went back to the hotel, dragging his feet, and Annette went on into the house.

There was a crowd of strangers in the lobby, and Jinks ducked back and went around to the rear of the hotel and up the back stairway. He didn't want another reception.

He paused outside Aunt Tish's door with his hand raised to knock. This was going to be painful. Before he could bring himself to knock, a door across the hall opened, and John Iverson stood in the doorway, studying him.

"Hi!" Jinks nodded coldly. Iverson nodded back.

Then Jinks noticed that Iverson had a small revolver in his hand, a shiny nickel-trimmed one. He wasn't pointing the weapon at Jinks. He was just twirling it on his index finger.

"Like to have a talk with you, Bradley." John Iverson spoke softly. "Come in a minute."

"Why, I was—uh—my aunt wants me to—" Jinks was fascinated by the revolver. And as he stared at it, the weapon came to a stop in its twirling and the barrel pointed directly at him.

"This way, please." Iverson smiled thinly and gestured with the weapon. "It won't take long."

Jinks wanted to say, "I'll see you later," but the words died in his throat. There was something about the expression of Iverson's eyes. . . .

Jinks crossed the hallway, and Iverson moved back a step to let him go past into the room. Then, after a hasty glance up and down the corridor, Iverson followed him in and closed the door.

CHAPTER 13

Accused

Annette had had a restful nap and was wide-awake and getting hungry. She was disappointed to find the house still silent. There was no sign of the family. They should be coming along home now, almost any time, with the Navajos who had signed up to do the roofing at the station.

She waited on the porch for Aunt Tish and Jinks to come over. By now, Aunt Tish would have forgiven him for speeding and spoiling her posters. She never stayed angry with him long.

She stared suddenly. Aunt Tish was striding over from the hotel. And Jinks wasn't with her. "Maybe she's locked him in his room for being naughty!" Annette chuckled secretly. But after one close look at Aunt Tish's grim expression, she sobered.

"The desk clerk tells me he saw Jinks in your car this afternoon. Where is my nephew?"

Annette thought, Uh-oh! He weakened and ran off! But aloud she asked, "Why, I thought he was with you. Didn't he tell you where he's been?"

"I haven't seen him! And what's more, Sheriff Martinez is looking for him. There's no use of his hiding. The whole mess has come out!" Aunt Tish was angry.

Annette stared at her, amazed. "What mess? Why is the sheriff looking for Jinks?"

"Because Jinks and Mr. Kerry have swindled Mr. Iverson by pretending that they found silver ore! They've 'salted' a claim and sold him an interest in it, Sheriff Martinez says."

"But Jinks didn't do any such thing—and neither did Mr. Kerry!" Annette was horrified. "You must believe me. It's all a horrible mistake—or a deliberate lie. Jinks never told anybody he'd

found any silver ore! He only had one piece—
and he bought that from an old miner named
Pete! He told me all about it. Honestly!"

Aunt Tish looked relieved for a moment, then
she shook her head sadly. "I'm afraid he didn't
tell you the truth, dear."

"I *know* he did! All of it." Annette's eyes
sparked with anger. "And if you'll just listen—"

"Why did he run away, if he didn't have a
guilty conscience? Where is he hiding now?"
Aunt Tish demanded.

"I don't know where he is now. But he didn't
run away the other day. He had an accident and
wrecked his car. And I bet that's the only reason
he isn't around right now—he's afraid you'll
scold him!" Annette cried.

Aunt Tish sighed and sat down heavily on the
steps. "I wish it were that simple, Annette. He
could wreck two cars and I'd still forgive him.
But to cheat someone—" She shook her head
unhappily.

An old truck was pulling up outside the Kerry
house. It was loaded with chairs and cartons of

things. Mr. Kerry was driving, and Mrs. Kerry was sitting beside him.

And as Lon Kerry maneuvered to drive the truck up to the old barn behind the house, Lisa called, "Come on, help us unload!"

But as Annette started to go around toward the barn, Aunt Tish stopped her with a hand on her arm. A tall figure had come from across the street and was going up the driveway after the truck. The big-brimmed hat and the loose-jointed walk were Sheriff Martinez's. "Let's give the sheriff a chance to tell Mr. Kerry what he's found out. Might be better not to be standing around listening."

But Annette shook off Aunt Tish's hand. "The Kerrys are my friends. I know Mr. Kerry wouldn't do anything wrong, any more than Jinks would! Lisa and I were with him when he found that ore out on the hill where we staked out the claims. We saw him find it! And I'm going to tell the sheriff so—and that nasty John Iverson, too!"

She rushed up the driveway after the sheriff.

Sheriff Martinez was finding it hard to bring

himself to tell his old friend why he had come to see him. The Kerrys were so happy over their recent good luck.

"Something on your mind, Tim?" Lon Kerry asked with a smile.

"Afraid so," the sheriff admitted. "I have some bad news for you."

Annette ran up to them. "Sheriff! Please—" She took hold of his sleeve. "It's all a silly mistake! Mr. Kerry didn't cheat that Iverson character, and neither did Jinks! Mr. Iverson is wrong!"

Before Martinez could speak, Lon Kerry wheeled on him, frowning. "What's this all about, Tim? What is Iverson claiming?"

The sheriff gulped. "Can't we go over to my office and discuss it there?" He had noticed Mrs. Kerry and Lisa hurrying over with shocked expressions.

"What's wrong, Dad?" Lisa asked quickly as she and her mother came up to them.

"I'm trying to find out," her father told her grimly. Then he turned to Sheriff Martinez. "You can tell me here. I have nothing to hide from my family or friends. Speak up, man!"

With a sigh, Sheriff Martinez told him what Iverson was charging.

"But it was Iverson himself who told me where someone had noticed the Bradley boy digging the day before!" Kerry was still too shocked to be angry. "Doesn't he remember that?"

"That's right." Annette backed him up. "He even lent Mr. Kerry his car to go look around there." She turned triumphantly to Lisa. "Didn't he?"

"He certainly did!" Lisa snapped.

Sheriff Martinez only looked more gloomy. "Sure. So he said. Only he says that seeing the kid out there, like this other fellow did, proves that young Bradley was salting the ground with ore so you could go out there and make a big deal out of finding it."

Lon Kerry wiped his forehead. He was a just man. He could see how it would look to Iverson, to the sheriff himself, to everyone. He felt sick. "But it wasn't like that."

"It's hard to believe, Lon. I'm trying not to,

and you know it. But Iverson's got evidence. And it looks like it's proof enough of what he claims."

"Evidence? How can he have evidence of something that never happened?" Lon Kerry demanded angrily.

"He has the boy's wristwatch that the two of you gave old Pete the Prospector—in return for the sack of silver ore that you used to spread around on that hill where you and the girls found it." Martinez was unhappy that he had to do this. "I saw the watch."

"Sack of ore? Old Pete?" Lon Kerry was bewildered now. "I don't know what you're talking about."

Annette couldn't keep quiet any longer. "Jinks did buy some ore with his wristwatch, Mr. Kerry. But it was only one chunk, the piece of rock he gave Lisa as a birthday present. He told me all about it this afternoon." She faced the sheriff with an assured smile.

"He admitted it was paid for with his watch?" Martinez asked gravely.

"Why, of course!" Annette cried. "But it was just one chunk! The old miner said it was worth more than the watch, and Jinks believed him and swapped. You can ask Jinks."

"This is all over my head!" Lon Kerry was getting angry now. "Where is the boy? Let's get hold of him and find out what's going on. I don't like being accused of crooked dealing just for some silly joke of his!" He glared at Martinez.

But Martinez shook his head morosely. "The boy has run away. That seems to prove he has something to hide."

"But it doesn't mean I'm mixed up in it! All I did was find the ore. I had no idea he had put it there!"

The sheriff was silent. He shuffled his feet on the graveled driveway. Then, he added, "Mr. Iverson says old Pete came to him when he was looking around the claim this morning. Pete laughed at him for buying into the claim and told him that *both* you and Jinks visited his camp on Deer Mountain and bought the ore with Jinks's watch."

"But I haven't been near Deer Mountain since the hunting season closed last year! The old man is lying! Where is he? I'll face him right now and make him admit it."

"Haven't seen him. But it's all set down on the paper he wrote for Iverson and sold to him for ten dollars." Martinez looked grim. "And Iverson got the watch for another ten."

Lon Kerry held his hand across his eyes. Things were coming too fast and hard for him. Lisa was pale, and her mother looked grief-stricken. But Annette's eyes flashed angrily.

"Anybody can make a statement. It doesn't have to be true," she told Sheriff Martinez.

"Maybe it isn't," Martinez admitted, "but John Iverson sure believes it, Miss Annette. He's raving mad about being cheated! Says he's going to get back every cent of his money or send Lon here and the Bradley boy to jail!" He turned to Lon. "Maybe if you came over and talked to him, Lon—he's in my office now—"

"Good! I'll come with you right now!" Kerry patted his wife's shoulder and tried to smile.

"Honey, don't you girls try to unpack the truck tonight. I'll have Thomas Yazzie and the other Navajos here in the morning, and they can tend to it. I'll be back soon, when I straighten out Iverson."

They watched him and the sheriff go down the driveway and disappear in the direction of the sheriff's office.

"Annette," Lisa whispered as Aunt Tish and Mrs. Kerry walked ahead of them toward the door, "do you think that Jinks *did*—?" She couldn't finish it.

She didn't have to. "Of course, I don't! Jinks may be young and childish, compared to some people, but he can look people in the eye without making their spines crawl! And that's more than I can say for John Iverson! Jinks is decent and honest. And so's your father. And Iverson can show all the confessions and stuff that he can buy from greedy old miners, and it will still be a lie!" It was a long speech, but she meant every word of it, and Lisa knew it and felt relieved.

* * *

But over in the sheriff's office, confronted and angrily accused by John Iverson, Lon Kerry could see that Sheriff Martinez was beginning to believe the younger man's story. It seemed to make sense.

"But it isn't true, Iverson!" he argued. "Look at it calmly. You're the one who put me on the track, told me where to look! My daughter heard you at the station!"

Iverson laughed scornfully. "I merely said someone had seen the boy in a general neighborhood out there. *You* pinpointed it"—he gave a sneering chuckle—"with no difficulty at all! And your daughter took her friend along to be sure someone saw you discover it!"

"Why, you—" Lon Kerry swung his fist so suddenly that the younger man had no chance to duck. It caught Iverson on the side of the jaw and staggered him.

Before he could recover, Sheriff Martinez had stepped between them. "That's enough! Hold it!" He kept Iverson back with one strong arm, while he waved back Kerry with the other.

"Calm down, Lon. Losing your temper won't help. And as for you, Iverson, watch yourself. Keep the girl out of it. You have no evidence against her."

Lon Kerry nursed his knuckles and glared at Iverson. But Iverson merely straightened his tie and shrugged.

"Okay," Iverson told Sheriff Martinez. "I'm sorry I spoke out of turn. But I intend to see that both Mr. Kerry and Jinks Bradley are held to answer for their faking. And I rather imagine the town of Pine Mesa will agree with any sentence a judge hands out."

"Now wait a minute, Mr. Iverson," the sheriff protested. "Mr. Kerry's a respected citizen. You're basing your charge on pretty flimsy evidence. Why don't you let him give back your thousand dollars and call it square? If anybody did anything crooked, it was the kid. And we'll find him soon."

"Well—" Iverson had seen that truckload of goods being brought in and had made it his business to learn that Kerry had bought the roofing.

"I might—if he hands it over first thing in the morning and makes a statement to my lawyer, admitting the fraud."

Lon Kerry stood up straight. "I won't sign a lying statement. I had no part in any fraud."

"But, Lon—maybe if you give him back the money right now—" Martinez was anxious to see it settled.

"That's something I couldn't do, even if I wanted to," Kerry said soberly. "I've spent most of it for repairs on the station and for that truck-load of curios."

"Maybe in a few days you could raise it—" Sheriff Martinez was almost coaxing him. "How about it, Iverson? Can you give him a little time to make it up? Keep things quiet a few days?"

Iverson walked to the window and stared out. The sun was almost gone. The street was bathed in a golden glow. It seemed a good omen. Things were going just the way he had planned and hoped.

He turned to Kerry and the sheriff. "I'm afraid not. But I have an alternative to offer you, Kerry. And I advise you to accept it."

CHAPTER 14

Defeat

Annette stood with Lisa down by the gate. They had been waiting for what seemed like ages for Mr. Kerry to come back from Sheriff Martinez's office. But the sun had set now and the streetlights were on, and there was still no sign of him.

Suddenly, Annette pointed down the street toward the office. "Why, there they go now! Mr. Iverson and your dad and Sheriff Martinez. Wonder where they're going."

Lisa craned her neck to look past the groups of people strolling through the street and shopping in the stores. She stepped up on the crossbar of the gate to look over their heads. "They're

181

stopping at the station!" she reported. "Now they're going in!"

"What on earth for? I wonder," Annette said, puzzled. "Maybe they think Jinks is hiding there! I'm going to see what's going on. Come on!"

The front gate of the station was open when they got there, and the big main house was deserted. But Annette heard the men's voices out in the courtyard, and she motioned to Lisa to be quiet, as they hurried on tiptoe across to the door and looked out.

Mr. Kerry, Iverson, and the sheriff were standing in the center of the courtyard, but there was no sign of Jinks. And they didn't seem to be searching for him, after all, Annette noticed with relief.

Then she heard Iverson, with a sharp edge to his voice, saying, "I want those Indians off this property by sunset tomorrow. I'll leave it to you to see to it."

Lisa looked at her, shocked. "What does he mean by giving orders about the station?" she whispered to Annette.

"Looks like he's finally persuaded your dad to sell it to him," Annette said, frowning.

"Oh, Dad would never do that! Unless— unless he—" She bogged down, scared suddenly as she realized that he might have had to.

"Unless John Iverson clubbed him into it, you mean!" Annette's eyes flashed with anger. "I bet that's just what happened!"

"They're coming this way!" Lisa was panicky.

"Come on!" Annette grabbed her hand, and they ran lightly across the room and out the front door, ducking into the shadows behind the tall shrubbery.

The men were coming through the big room now.

"I'd better take that statement of old Pete's, Iverson. I'm sending my deputy to Deer Mountain to bring in Pete tomorrow for questioning," the sheriff was saying.

Iverson laughed. "I think it's safer with me. I'll be glad to let you borrow it—when you find him."

"Okay," Sheriff Martinez agreed. "May take a

few days to locate him, at that. He's always on the move."

The three men moved past the girls, who held their breath and crouched as low as they could.

The men stood talking in low tones on the sidewalk. Then Annette heard Iverson say, "We'll sign the papers tomorrow morning. And I want to take possession as soon as the Indians get out."

"All right, Iverson. But you're mistaken about this thing, and I expect to prove it to you before long." Mr. Kerry sounded pretty downhearted in spite of his brave words.

The sheriff and Iverson went on up the street, but Lon Kerry stood with slumped shoulders. Lisa jumped up and ran to throw her arms around the startled man's neck. "Dad! What's going on? Why is Mr. Iverson giving orders about the station?"

Annette thought she had a pretty good idea without being told. And when Kerry explained, it turned out to be just about as she had expected. Iverson had agreed not to charge Kerry and Jinks

with fraud, but in return for his silence, and a check for another thousand drawn on his Coast bank, he was to take the station at once.

Lisa was heartbroken as she and her father went down the street together. But Annette was angry. It seemed to her that John Iverson had managed some trick to get what he had been wanting all along—the stage station.

Maybe the sheriff would catch up with Pete tomorrow. The old man would have to tell the truth and clear both Jinks and Mr. Kerry.

But where was Jinks? And why was he hiding? She stayed awake a long time after the Kerry house was silent that night. Lisa had been stunned at the loss of the station and all the high hopes they had for it. She had cried softly in the dark and finally had fallen asleep from exhaustion. But Annette paced the floor in her bare feet and stared out the window at the noisy newcomers who were wandering around out in the street.

When she did tumble into bed at last, she had made up her mind to go looking for Jinks herself. There was one place where he might be hiding—

the old mine on the hill above the claims. She would slip away early and find out if her hunch was a good one.

She slept later than she had planned, and by the time she came down to breakfast, the others had finished. Mr. Kerry was at the lawyer's office, meeting John Iverson.

Lisa and her mother had gone over to the station to gather together a few personal belongings that had somehow drifted over there in the past few months of running back and forth. Some of Lisa's friends were helping.

Aunt Tish, rocking on the porch, was waiting for Annette to come down.

"I don't know why I overslept!" Annette was cross with herself. "Has Jinks showed up yet?"

"No sign of him," Aunt Tish snapped. "I'm ashamed of him, Annette."

There was no use trying to think of excuses, Annette knew. She started to say, "I'm going to look for him," but she only got as far as "I'm going . . ." when she realized that Aunt Tish might want to go along. And Jink's aunt would jump all over Jinks if they found him. So she just finished, "I'm going to ride out and see what's going on at the claim."

Annette went down to the livery stable and hired a horse. There were a lot of them around now, and she wouldn't be so noticeable on horse-back as she would be in her white car.

The hillside was all laid out with claim notices, and there were quite a few people hope-fully searching for signs of the wealth they had come to find. They were cheerful and enthusias-tic. But there were others, not far away, who wore sullen and angry expressions as they kicked away their discovery stakes and started packing up to leave.

Annette tied her horse to a sapling near the foot of the hill and toiled up the slope.

There was a warning sign near the boarded-up entrance to the mine: PRIVATE PROPERTY KEEP OFF. But Annette went around the side of the hill, picking a bunch of lupine and yellow poppies, and moving gradually up toward the ramshackle cluster of old buildings.

She was within fifty feet of a tumbledown shed when she saw the hat. Her heart went up into her throat, and she stood staring at it. It was a straw hat with a red band. It was exactly like the one that Jinks had been wearing when she saw him last! It was lying on the ground near the old shed.

She ran to it and picked it up. There was nothing to indicate whose hat it was—no initials inside, no special trimming except for the silly red band around it. But it *could* belong to Jinks. She hoped that it did.

She was cupping her hands to her mouth to call for Jinks when she noticed the sun reflecting off something inside the shed. There was a wide section of board missing there, and she cautiously approached to peer inside.

A huge tarpaulin-covered car stood in the shed, with the sun glinting on a long section of chrome-plated bumper. It was a big convertible.

Pretty fancy car for a prospector! Annette thought. But maybe it doesn't belong to any prospector. Maybe it's Iverson's! And maybe—

maybe Jinks stole it to come up here and hide, if he has a guilty conscience! It was the first time she had let herself think for a moment that Jinks might have lied to her. It was a horrible thought.

She didn't want to believe it of Jinks, but she had to know if it was the truth. So she marched determinedly around the corner of the old shed in search of him—and came face-to-face with a giant of a man with a red beard.

He scowled forbiddingly at her. "Can't you read signs, missy? This place is private. Better run along and pick your posies someplace else!"

She took a backward step, staring fascinated at his mop of red hair. "I'm sorry!" she stammered, dropping part of her bouquet.

"Pick 'em up if you want 'em," he ordered.

But she didn't wait to pick up the flowers. She hurried away, still clutching the red-banded hat in one hand and the rest of the flowers in the other.

"Didn't mean to scare you, missy," his voice boomed out behind her. "Just tryin' to make sure you didn't hurt yourself wanderin' around this rusty old machinery or fallin' down an old shaft!"

She looked back fleetingly and saw his red whiskers split into a wide grin, as he waved good-naturedly after her. A gold tooth gleamed in the sun! It was Theresa's ghost, and very much alive!

So he *had* been hiding up there since he scared Charley that night at the station! And he must have been there, she thought, when John Iverson went up to find Theresa's lamb. Iverson had taken a long time about it. Maybe they knew each other. And maybe, if that was Iverson's car up there, Iverson was up there, too,

She hurried down the hill, thinking that had she met him, she would have told him what she thought of his accusing Mr. Kerry and Jinks!

Jinks! Apparently he wasn't at the mine, after all—even if the hat looked exactly like his. There must be dozens like it around. She tossed it carelessly aside and rode back to Pine Mesa, disappointed.

She had no way of knowing that, in the highest shack of the old mine buildings, Jinks Bradley was propped up against the wall, a gag in his mouth and his hands and feet tied.

CHAPTER 15

Annette Finds the Answer

All the way back to town, Annette kept hoping that Jinks had returned from wherever he had been hiding and had been able to convince the sheriff that it was all a mistake.

But when she stopped her mount outside the gate, to call to Lisa on the porch, Lisa hurried down to tell her there had been no word of Jinks. And Sheriff Martinez hadn't been able to find old Pete to question him. "He may be a hundred miles away in the hills by now," Lisa said wearily. "So, there's no use trying to track him down."

Lisa showed her the Flagstaff paper that had just been delivered. It made fun of Pine Mesa.

Annette read the headlines angrily. "'Pine Mesa's bid for fame only a publicity stunt to advertise new inn to be opened soon by "discoverer" Lon Kerry!'"

"It's so unfair!" Lisa was on the verge of tears. "Dad hasn't done a thing, and they're treating him like a criminal!"

"It's all John Iverson's fault!" Annette declared stormily. "If he hadn't made Jinks jealous—"

Lisa nodded in agreement.

Annette left to return the horse to the stables. When she returned she glanced across at the hotel and saw John Iverson, carrying two suitcases, come out and stride down the street toward the station. He seemed in a hurry as he briskly elbowed his way through groups of men standing around idle.

Annette thought resentfully, He isn't losing any time taking possession! And she wondered, as she had so many times, why he could possibly want to move into an old broken-down place like the station. Just stubborn, maybe. One of those "nobody can cross me" guys!

It was almost dark when Charley and his family came by from the station with their furniture piled high on a borrowed wagon. They drew up into the driveway. They were to spend the night and then go on back to the reservation in the morning.

But it was only Charley and Marie who went in at the kitchen door. Theresa was huddled on a pile of bedding at the rear of the wagon, and Esteban the lamb was bleating beside her. Annette went over to her and found her in tears. "Why, honey, what's the matter? Don't you want to take a nice trip?"

Theresa only wept harder, and the lamb baaed louder.

Annette put her arms around the sobbing child. "Tell me," she urged gently.

"My doll," Theresa sobbed. "The man would not let me look for my kachina doll. It's my good-luck doll because it was given to me by my family's Hopi friends. He sent us away. He said, 'You go now or I'll kick you out. This is *my* house now!'"

"Oh, he did, did he?" Annette's dark eyes flashed. "We'll see about that! We'll find your doll. And he'd better not try to kick *me* out!"

She helped Theresa out of the wagon, and they marched bravely down to the station. But when she tried the front door, it was locked, and there was no answer to her knock.

"There is a hole in the wall behind our house," the little girl whispered. "Let us go that way."

Annette couldn't help feeling that she would like to avoid arguing with John Iverson if possible. She didn't feel so brave, now that she was here. "Okay," she agreed, and they hurried around to the rear wall.

They got through easily, and raced to the dark little house where the Nez family had lived. It was only a few yards from the wall to the rear window of Theresa's bedroom.

The window opened easily, and Annette saw that the room was empty, its door closed. Theresa slipped off her shoes, with Annette's help, so she could move about without any noise, and Annette lifted her over the sill into the bedroom. "Not a sound now!" she cautioned, again in a whisper.

Theresa suppressed a giggle. "I'll look in the closet!" she whispered, and moved away along the dark wall.

There was a heavy step in the living room, and a moment later the door started to open. It was John Iverson! He was carrying a lamp in one hand and a long-handled ax in the other.

Theresa scurried into the darkness of the closet and pulled the door almost shut after her—seconds before Iverson was wholly inside the room! Annette waited only long enough to be sure Theresa was out of sight. Then she ducked down into the shrubbery below the window.

There was a sound of rending wood, the squeak of boards being forced apart. Then, an exclamation from Iverson. It sounded like "That's it!" and Annette couldn't resist one quick peek over the windowsill to see what had pleased him.

She was just in time to see him lowering

himself into a sizable hole in the floor—under a trapdoor he had just pried open. He disappeared, leaving the lamp on the edge of the hole.

Annette could see the closet door opening a little and Theresa's grinning face peering out. The little girl held up the kachina doll for her to see and started to come out. But, as she did, Annette saw something being lifted up out of the hole, and she wildly waved Theresa back into the closet.

As Theresa disappeared again, Annette saw that the object coming into view was a small, dusty nail keg. Iverson set it alongside the hole and then climbed out himself, as cobwebby and dusty as the keg.

He was looking the other way, so she watched him, fascinated, as he quickly knocked off the rusty hoops and wrenched apart the barrel staves.

Money spilled out! Neat packets of paper money, still bound by paper wrappers used by the banks, stamped with the amount they held.

Chuckling to himself, Iverson knelt beside the pile of currency and gloated over it. Then he started to stuff it into his pockets. In a minute he seemed to realize that he hadn't room for all of it. He came to a quick decision, took the lamp, and hurried out.

Annette heard him go out the front door and cross the courtyard with ringing steps, whistling as he went.

She climbed in through the window and hurried to the closet. Theresa, squatting contentedly on the floor there, was humming to her gaudily painted wooden doll as she rocked it in her arms. "Come! Let's go!" Annette urged.

Theresa scrambled to her feet, and Annette hurried her to the window.

"Wait!" Annette turned back and snatched up a thick bundle of the paper money. She brought it to the window and thrust it into the deep pocket of Theresa's wide skirt. "Take this to the sheriff! Quick! Understand?" she whispered urgently.

Theresa nodded. "Are you coming?"

"I think I'll wait around and see if he takes it away from here. I may want to follow him so I can tell the sheriff where to find him." She helped Theresa over the windowsill and onto the ground. "Tell the sheriff to come here right away! And show him that money!"

Annette watched her run through the hole in the wall. She was about to climb out herself when she heard Iverson's heavy footsteps rapidly crossing the living room floor.

She had just time to dart into the closet and close the door to a narrow crack before lamplight flooded in as Iverson entered, carrying a suitcase.

He set down the lamp, opened the suitcase, and, kneeling beside them, began to scoop up the money. It was almost all packed neatly in the suitcase when he heard something outside that made him rise quickly. A small revolver came out of his pocket, but at the sound of a low signal whistle, he thrust it back out of sight, scowling.

Hastily stuffing the rest of the money into the suitcase, he dropped the lid. Then he picked up the lamp and hurried out.

A couple of minutes passed and then Annette

heard voices in the living room. She recognized Shay's.

"I come to help you look," he was saying defiantly. "I got as much rights as you have. I don't have to sit up there at that blasted mine and wait! How do I know you won't run off with it like your pa did? Yeah—an' leave me to take the blame for kidnappin'!'"

"I've already found the money, and I was just coming up to the mine to split it with you!" Iverson was angry.

Annette moved quickly. She darted out, emptied the suitcase into the black hole in the floor, and got it back to its place with the lid down. She disappeared into the closet a split second before the men came in with the lamp.

"Did you leave the Bradley kid tied up in the shack?" Iverson was asking.

"Yeah. Real tight!" Shay was looking at the suitcase. "Is it in there?" He started over toward it. "Let's have the split now. I been waitin' twenty years to get my hands on that loot!"

"We can wait till we're clear of here," Iverson

snapped. He reached the suitcase before Shay could and picked it up. As he did, it fell open, and one thin bundle, which had stuck in a corner, fell to the floor.

"Oh, yeah?" Shay grabbed the empty suitcase. "What's your trick now?" He pulled out a knife. "Where you hidin' it this time?"

But Iverson was just as surprised as Shay. He stood staring stupidly at the empty suitcase. Then Shay flung aside the suitcase and came at him, reaching for him with one hand and threatening with the knife.

Iverson came out of his daze and sidestepped. Then he brought up a hard fist that landed on Shay's chin, staggering him.

Iverson tried to draw his revolver, but Shay was at him. They struggled around the room, narrowly escaping the open hole to the tunnel and missing the lamp on the floor by inches.

Annette watched tensely through the crack of the door and wished hard that the sheriff would get there before there was any bloodshed.

She got her wish. Iverson had finally forced

the bigger man to drop the knife and was reaching for his own weapon, when Sheriff Martinez's
voice commanded, "Hold it right there, Iverson!
You're both under arrest!"

The sheriff strode in, followed by his deputy,
both with drawn guns. Lon Kerry was right
behind them.

As the law officers lined up the desperate
men to search and disarm them, Lon Kerry
demanded, "Where is Annette?" He confronted
Iverson threateningly. "If you've harmed her—"

Annette came out of the closet. "I'm all right,
Mr. Kerry. Just a little scared, that's all. You'll
find Jinks at the mine." She faced the downcast
Iverson and Shay. "They kidnapped him!"

Later, in the sheriff's office, Iverson was
tight-lipped and grim, but Shay was ready to
talk. He told the whole story, going back twenty
years to the robbery of the Tucson bank. Now
there were more headlines in the making for Pine
Mesa, but good ones this time!

They found Jinks at the mine, unharmed but stiff

and sore from being tied up so long. The town made a hero of him all over again when they found out that it was his suggestion to Gold-Tooth Shay, as they sat it out up there, that had made the big man come charging down to demand his share of the loot at once from Iverson. If the two schemers hadn't fought, they might have escaped.

Annette was acclaimed, too, and Theresa came in for a share of the limelight, which she thoroughly enjoyed.

There was to be a reward for the recovery of the money. Moldy though most of it turned out to be after twenty years underground, it was still legal tender and worth its full face value.

But no one seemed sure who would get the five-hundred-dollar reward. Would it be Annette— or Jinks—or would the money be divided?

Annette and Jinks couldn't wait around to find out. They, along with Lisa, were due back on the Coast for school on Monday. And besides, the two of them had a little secret about that reward money: they were going to invest it in the

Kerrys' pet project, the inn. They hadn't told this to anyone except an approving Aunt Tish. It was to be a surprise for the Kerrys!

They sat on the porch steps Saturday night, surrounded by Lisa's friends, now their friends, too. They sang and talked and were often silent, thinking of tomorrow when they would be going away.

In the big kitchen, Aunt Tish was having her last pot of tea with the Kerrys. There was no thought of their giving up the station now. John Iverson had been forced to confess that the check he had given in payment had been drawn on a bank where he had no funds.

Outside, the kids were singing softly about the Red River Valley and the sadness of parting, and Jinks was holding Lisa's hand right out in front of everyone.

Billy Joe and Dave were trying hard to persuade Annette to come back for the Christmas holidays, and she was promising to try. Maybe Aunt Lila and Uncle Archie would come along with her.

Later, after their friends had left, Mr. Kerry

told Annette and Jinks, while Lisa listened happily, "We'll make out all right now. The bank
will carry us for whatever we need to finish the
inn. Our publicity has boomed business in Pine
Mesa!"

And Mrs. Kerry, hugging Annette, added,
"And it all happened because you brought our
girl home to spend the holiday with us!"

Next morning, with Aunt Tish beside her and
Lisa and Jinks following, Annette drove home-
ward feeling content. There had been some
rough moments, but all in all, it had been a wonderful desert holiday!